THE MAN IN THE FIELD

PRAISE FOR JAMES COOPER

"It's been quite a while since I've encountered stories like this, tales that ignore topical tastes in favour of a strange view of humanity that's timeless, classical and mysteriously sad."

—Christopher Fowler, author of *The Bryant & May Series*

"James Cooper's work is odd. It is edgy, individual, outspoken. It is steeped in a knowledge of and love for horror fiction that informs every line. It has, above all, a quality of unnerving weirdness that makes you question what you know of the world."

—Nina Allan, author of *The Dollmaker*

THE MAN IN THE FIELD

James Cooper

Cemetery Dance Publications
Baltimore
2022

Cemetery Dance Publications
Baltimore, MD
2022

Cemetery Dance Publications
132-B Industry Lane, Unit #7
Forest Hill, MD 21050
CemeteryDance.com

ISBN: 978-1-58767-825-7

For Anna and Ethan.

And the dark star that was Shirley Jackson…

FOREWORD:
"WHAT THE HELL HAPPENS NEXT?"

LIKE most writers, I often wonder about the life that might exist—that *must* exist, I suppose—for characters I've created once the final full stop has been applied at the end of a story.

Unless the protagonist dies on the last page, there has to be a fictional life beyond that of the one that's been described by the author. That's surely a given. Most stories, long or short, will arrive at some pre-determined resolution point, but that doesn't mean that the character's journey is over. There is always another chapter, the next step taken, an untold tale to be recounted.

Characters live independently of the story, all writers are eminently conscious of this, which is why you will often hear them talk of losing control of what a character might say or do within the context of the story. This idea of characters assuming autonomous agency, somehow shaping their lives and determining their own outcome, has always fascinated me. I am a writer who believes implicitly that meticulous plotting of a story is futile when you're dealing with characters into whom you've—hopefully—breathed real life and who are invested in their own sense of narrative freedom. They have histories and back-stories; and if this is the case, they must surely have undisclosed futures, too, destinies that neither the author nor the reader can see, but which both know almost certainly exist, out there somewhere in the vast fictional space from which characters and their ongoing stories are drawn.

This brings me via a rather circuitous route to *The Man in the Field* and the evolution of what was originally a three-thousand-word story written for a collection of mine entitled *Scar Tissue*, published earlier this year by PS Publishing.

That initial short story is essentially the first chapter of the expanded version you now hold in your hands. The question, I suppose, that is most obvious from a reader's point of view is why did I feel the need to develop a story that was—as far as these things ever can be—already resolved and locked in to another project altogether? To which my immediate answer would be, what makes you think I had a choice?

Those people who read the original short story provided positive feedback and generally loved the strange world that I had created in *The Man in the Field*; but nearly all of them finished reading the tale and, after due consideration, sent me a message asking, "What the hell happens next?"

It was a question that had been plaguing me, too. Mother Tanner and Father Lynch, even in such a relatively short space, had acquired compelling lives of their own and had taken root beyond my imagination. Or so it seemed. My mind kept drifting back to this short tale—which I had originally written as a tribute to Shirley Jackson as part of my love letter to a handful of great genre writers—urging me to consider what steps these characters might have taken next. I knew that something must have happened, I just didn't know what. Not yet, at least. These characters had assumed an independent agency that all writers pray for, but are also mildly alarmed to detect, forever afraid that this very freedom might adversely affect the story into which they've been placed.

I let the matter pass, trusting that this tale and these characters would find their own path and create their own invisible trail, without the need for me to bear witness to it.

Strangely, though, on this particular occasion this proved not to be the case. I caught a glimpse of the destinies awaiting both Mother Tanner and Father Lynch, and the compulsion to investigate where this might lead was too great to resist. There was another story to be told here, a richer story, one that took the original premise and allowed the characters involved to grow and reveal themselves in more detail to both me and the reader. All I had to do was turn them loose; the story essentially took care of itself from that moment on.

The net result, some thirty-thousand-words later, was a novella that explored in intimate detail the relationship between Mother Tanner and the peculiar community that had shaped her life. During the course of the writing, I discovered, much to my relief, that I had answered the pressing question of what happens next, only to realize that I was working towards a similar conundrum at the end of the new, expanded tale—that same question, always surfacing: "what happens next?"—feeling constantly like I was chasing the narrative into a black hole.

This is because, no matter how complete the story might seem, there is always more to be told. As noted earlier, the only clear resolution to any narrative is the death of the protagonist, and even this leaves much to be speculated upon: the impact on those left behind, the ongoing ripples of grief, the traumatic process of trying to move on…

But for now all I have to share with you is a small part of Mother Tanner's journey, this odd little tale of sacrifice and resilience in the shadow of a dystopian society. That's not to say, of course, that this is all there was, or all there will be. Just that, at the moment, this is all I know.

Against this backdrop, we must respect the mysterious ritual of drawing from the story-pool; peering into the depths only ever reveals a fragment of the tale. What the darkness below holds is anybody's guess…

James Cooper
Nottinghamshire
December 15, 2021

CHAPTER 1

THE man in the field arrived, as was his custom, on the first day of the Spring Equinox. It was Mother Tanner who saw him first, standing in the middle of Father Miller's newly-ploughed field, his face turned towards the trees. He was wearing a white suit and black leather boots, though these were planted firmly in the earth. He looked, Mother Tanner thought, like a minister giving a lonely sermon to the circling birds above.

She dropped the sack of grain she had collected from the barn and peered into the middle distance, wanting to make sure she hadn't mistaken the man in the field for one of Father Miller's farmhands. No, there he was; large as life, with his black felt hat worn at a jaunty angle to partially hide his face. He was leaner than Mother Tanner remembered, as though in the year since she'd last set eyes on him the man had grown spindle-thin. He looked like he needed a good meal, Mother Tanner thought, and the idea made her wince as she considered the amount of food the villagers would consume later in the day to celebrate the Turning of the Wheel.

She was still the only one in the vicinity and it occurred to her that no one else knew that the man in the field had returned. For the moment, she had him all to herself. She felt strangely exhilarated, as though she'd been caught doing something unseemly. Her cheeks colored and she could hear the beating of her heart in her chest. There he was, standing alone in the field, staring at the woodland beyond. He was everything and nothing; a white scarecrow wearing a black felt hat. How she yearned to see his face, just once, just to behold whatever inhabited his eyes.

The moment passed and she heard Father Miller close the door of the chicken coop and wander over to join her by the barn. He had a basket full of eggs hooked over his left arm.

"Regular as clockwork," he said, staring at the man in the field. "Reckon he must hear the first seed we sow."

Mother Tanner nodded, but knew it wasn't so much the seeds as the grinding of the Wheel. This was the time for regeneration, for encouraging new growth, that was the top and bottom of it. The Wheel rolled on, the crops were planted, and the man in the field returned.

"We should inform the others," Father Miller said, but made no move to do so; he just stared towards the horizon at the man in the perfectly laundered white suit.

A noise from behind startled them and they both turned to see Mother Gilmore holding a hand to her mouth. Her white prayer cap sat crookedly atop her head.

"I guess we should be used to him by now," she said, "but honest to goodness, my feelings on the matter never change. That man is about as welcome as a wet shoe!"

Mother Tanner covered the short distance between them and laid a hand on Mother Gilmore's arm. "You shouldn't say such things," she whispered. "He might hear you. Do you really want to draw attention to yourself that way?"

Mother Gilmore adjusted her prayer cap and felt a sudden heat rise in her cheeks. "Of course not. It's just that it's about time someone—"

The sound of heavy boots scrabbling across the dirt broke Mother Gilmore's train of thought. When both ladies looked up they saw Father Lynch striding towards them, a large grin spread across his face.

"Ah! I wondered when our benefactor would arrive. I even woke up this morning thinking about him. Imagine that! A small part of me was beginning to wonder if he'd forsaken us."

"Would that be such a bad thing?" Mother Gilmore muttered, drawing a look of alarm from Father Lynch.

"Perhaps you would prefer a year of crop failure and blighted harvest," he said sharply. "You would wish suffering upon your family and friends?"

Mother Gilmore lowered her eyes, naturally deferring to Father Lynch's conspicuous position in the community. As one of the village elders, it was only right that he was duly respected, though Mother Tanner could see that Mother Gilmore extended him this courtesy with nothing more than the faintest bow of the head.

Father Lynch allowed the moment to pass and summoned Father Miller's eldest son Michael from the nearby farmhouse.

"See that everyone knows that the man in the field has returned. Go from house to house, spreading the word. Tell everyone to join us here within the hour."

Michael nodded and ran off down the path, thrilled to have been chosen to broadcast the good news to their neighbors. He knew that some of them would be terribly afraid. There would be curses as he flitted from door to door. They might smile and nod politely to his face, but their blessings when he left would be hollow. They all knew why the man in the field had come, why he *had* to come. This was how the village worked. It was how the village had *always* worked. There was nothing anyone could say or do to make it stop.

THE VILLAGERS assembled in Father Miller's yard, all rushing to gaze upon the motionless figure of the man in the field. There was a murmur of excitement running through the small crowd as they jostled for the best view. Mother Tanner noticed that several of the women carrying small babies also wore straw amulets depicting the Wheel; they looked solemnly towards the man in the white suit.

As was the established practice, Mother Leslie had organized half a dozen of her cooking club to put on a spread for the occasion. Father Miller had laid out two foldaway tables and the ladies were busily arranging sandwiches, pastries and a variety of fruit and vegetables for the villagers to enjoy. Mother Stonehill was in charge of drinks and was dispensing fruit juice to the children and homemade wine to the flustered parents. Off by the barn, Father Benton was seated on an overturned crate, quietly playing 'Oh, Sweet Ear of Corn' on a scuffed violin to an audience of infatuated girls.

"It comes round so fast," Mother Dalton said, startling Mother Tanner out of her reverie. "Hard to imagine that a whole year has passed."

Mother Tanner smiled and nodded, though in truth she felt a little awkward. It had been during last year's celebration that Mother Dalton's daughter, Flora, had slipped away, taking her six-month-old daughter and everything she owned and losing herself in the fever of the big city. Mother Dalton hadn't heard from her since.

"It's good to see you here, Louise," Mother Tanner said, and Mother Dalton offered a faint smile, then turned her head and stared off towards the lowering sun.

Mother Tanner moved on through the crowd, acknowledging people as she went, a smile here, a courtly nod there, always quick to extend a steadying hand as the children ran laughing through the busy yard.

She noticed several boys who had discreetly advanced towards the edge of Father Miller's field. They had a handful of stones and were taking careful aim at the man in the field, whose unprotected back seemed an easy, if rather distant, target. As she watched, Mother Leslie, ever the guardian of moral integrity, strode towards them wielding a large ladle; wisely, the boys dropped the stones and ran for cover in the nearby trees.

"Seems to get busier every year," Mother Saunders said with a sigh. "I swear this village will outgrow itself before too long. Then where will we be?"

"A village is only as strong as the people in it, Hilda. Think of it this way: the place is richer for having all these children running around. Imagine how dull the place would be without them."

Mother Saunders did not look convinced. "If only the brutes were a little more civilized," she said. "Is that too much to ask, Helen?"

Mother Tanner laughed and continued on her way, easing herself through the crowd. She watched the children shrieking and dancing in the yard; how happy they look, she thought. The boys, in keeping with tradition, were wearing black felt hats and turning their backs on each other, mimicking the man they had come here to honor. Not to be denied their own tribute, many of the girls were carrying straw dollies, some of which had been dressed in simple white suits, skillfully woven from string. She smiled at the innocence of it and cast her eyes once more towards the real thing, the setting sun throwing a lengthy shadow behind the man in the field, who, as always, remained rooted to the spot.

She stood at the edge of the yard, thinking of the strange ritual they had chosen to observe. She felt a presence beside her and turned to see the plain, dough-like face of Mother Cullen, her newborn baby held tightly to her chest. The girl was no more than seventeen and Mother Tanner knew that the child had been the unwelcome gratuity left by a boy from a neighboring town. Mother Cullen claimed not to know his name nor had any interest in tracking him down. She was, she said, perfectly content to live her life alone in the village with her son. It had been a difficult time, Mother Tanner recalled; the girl's friends had disowned her and many of the villagers looked away when they saw her walking her child in the street. Had it not been for Father Whittaker taking her in and giving her and the baby a room, Mother Cullen would have had no choice but to leave the village. Even this had been fraught with challenges, the gossip-mongers finding much to deride in an elderly widow sharing a house with a young woman of questionable virtue.

Mother Tanner raised her hand and tickled the baby under its chin.

"What a gorgeous child," she said. "You must wake up every morning, take a look at this little fellow and consider yourself blessed."

Mother Cullen smiled and the simple pleasure that appeared on her face transformed her features. She looks beautiful, Mother Tanner thought; tired, anxious even, but undoubtedly made more attractive because of her love for the dribbling creature in her arms.

They gazed at the child for a moment and then they both looked up and stared absently at the man in the field.

"He never seems to change," Mother Cullen said. "The same from one year to the next."

"It would seem so."

Mother Cullen stroked her son's hair and said, "Has anybody ever seen his face?"

The question shocked Mother Tanner, though she couldn't quite articulate why. After all, wasn't that the only question worth asking?

"I have no idea," she said, surprised that there weren't countless apocryphal tales of intrepid young men keen to find out for themselves the answer to that very question. "I suppose we grow up being told how grateful we should be that his attention is on something else."

Mother Tanner cast her eyes to the right and saw Father Lynch slipping away through the crowd. Not long now, then; they would all be giving thanks soon enough.

"Would you like to hold him?" Mother Cullen said, offering the swaddled baby. Mother Tanner hesitated and then held out her arms. The child looked up at her and she marveled at how earnest he seemed, his eyes blinking away the light.

"Beautiful," she said, handing him back. "Quite beautiful."

Mother Cullen's face glowed with pride. "Not everyone seems to think so," she said. "Some people can't even bring themselves to look at him."

"That's because some people have no soul," Mother Tanner said softly, and Mother Cullen laughed.

There was a loud rapping behind them, coming from the space at the front of the yard. They turned round and saw Father Miller standing on a small podium. Everyone had stopped what they were doing to tend to his announcement.

"Such a large turnout," he said, smiling. "Please make a path for Father Lynch as he makes his way to the podium."

The crowd parted and Father Lynch wound his way from the farmhouse, through the throng and up onto the podium, where he beamed at his audience. He had changed from his tunic and breeches into a neatly-pressed white linen suit and a black felt hat. He looked, Mother Tanner thought, like a sinister version of the man to whom he was paying tribute.

"Welcome all to yet another confirmation of the planting season!" Father Lynch said, his powerful voice resonating around the yard. "How quickly it comes upon us. Another year where we have been blessed with high yields and the fulfilment of the harvest has come to pass!"

The crowd raised their hands and cheered and the wattage of Father Lynch's beam was nudged towards full power, much to Mother Tanner's disgust.

"Please join me in giving thanks for our bounty."

Mother Tanner watched as everyone lowered their heads and closed their eyes, before she too complied.

"Creator God, forgive our moments of ingratitude, the spiritual blindness that prevents us from appreciating the wonder that is this world, the endless cycle of nature, of life and death and rebirth. Forgive us for taking without giving, reaping without sowing. Open our eyes to see, our lips to praise, our hands to share. May our feet tread lightly on the path we choose and our footsteps be worthy of following. For they lead to you, now and forever. Amen."

Mother Tanner had heard the prayer before, but today it sounded less like an invocation and more like one of Father Lynch's moral discourses; not so much a prayer of thanks as a form of religious penance.

She opened her eyes and heard a hum of enthusiasm pass through the crowd. She peered through the bobbing heads and saw Father Miller wheeling in a small wooden cart. On top of it was a large tin of homemade whitewash, and resting on top of this was a new synthetic paintbrush, an item donated by Father Grelling from his store. The cart was guided towards the podium and then Father Miller retreated to the margins to allow Father Lynch to continue with his work.

"Okay children, who wants to come up here and give the wash one final stir?"

The children below the podium thrust their hands towards the sky and screamed their enthusiasm at him until their throats were raw. Father Lynch laughed and raised his hand in a vain attempt to calm them.

"Only one child gets the privilege," he said. "Who among you feels lucky?"

Apparently they all did. They leaped into the air, trying to catch Father Lynch's eye.

"Mother Daniels, why don't you choose? Who's worked especially hard in school?"

Mother Daniels smiled and looked at the upturned faces of the children. "So many to choose from this year," she said. "But Billy Gilmore has worked especially hard. The responsibility should be his."

Billy's face radiated happiness and he pushed his way to the front of the crowd and retrieved the wooden mixing rod from Father Lynch. He approached the cart with something close to reverence, his hands visibly trembling. Father Miller removed the brush and eased open the lid of the wash.

"Give it plenty of elbow grease, Billy!" Father Lynch advised. "This year's crops might depend on it!"

Some of the crowd broke into laughter and Mother Tanner couldn't help feeling disappointed in them. Father Lynch needed little enough encouragement as it was; laughing at his feeble attempt at humor only pumped up the wattage of his grin.

Billy lifted the mixing rod into the whitewash and began to gently give it a stir. The crowd cheered, roaring their support and laughing as he splashed some of it onto his clothes.

"Keep it in the tin, son!" Father Lynch barked, joining in the laughter.

Mother Gilmore slapped a hand to her forehead as she watched her son make a spectacle of himself with the wash, which only caused more amusement among the crowd.

Mother Tanner, who had seen this ritual performed on many occasions, turned away and trained her gaze on the man in the field instead. Light was fading from the sky and the distant woodland was now an imposing presence on the horizon. The man still hadn't moved; his back remained turned on proceedings in the yard and he stared only at a creeping darkness, his view impoverished by the black membrane settling across the land. What does he think about while he waits, she thought? What torments occupy his mind?

"How can he stand like that for so long?" Mother Cullen said, as though dipping into Mother Tanner's head and unpicking her thoughts. "It's unnatural."

It was hard to argue and Mother Tanner said nothing, allowing her silence to be answer enough.

There was a long pause, during which Mother Tanner could hear Father Lynch behind her continuing to entertain the crowd, before Mother Cullen said, "It's going to be different this time. For me, I mean. Is it wrong that I feel afraid?"

She rocked her baby in her arms and soothed him with a gentle, almost inaudible lullaby.

"Of course not," Mother Tanner said. "It's perfectly normal. If you weren't afraid, I'd think there was something wrong with you."

Mother Cullen smiled briefly, but was unable to cling on to it. "It's silly, I know, but I want the Wheel to turn and everything to go back to being just as it was. Like yesterday, and the day before that, and the day before that."

"Those days will return soon enough. They always do. You just have to be patient. Eventually, the man in the field will move on."

Mother Cullen nodded and they both turned to face Father Lynch as he began drawing the evening's celebrations to a close.

"Okay, folks. That about wraps it up for tonight. I shall leave you with one final thought, which I ask you to consider as you fall asleep in your partner's arms. These customs we practice have been passed down to us through the ages. They mark who we are and bring everlasting peace to our community. We place our trust in death and rebirth, as we know we must, because there is no regeneration without decay. Everything dies in its season; everything is reborn. This is the cycle we endure." He looked over the podium at the attentive crowd and lowered his voice. "Remember: the one marked by the white circle will be the one who makes a sacrifice for all."

NIGHT HAD finally fallen and the village lay in darkness. Father Miller's yard lay empty and silent, save for the errant twitching of a rusted weather vane on top of the barn. The tin of whitewash still rested on top of the cart but now looked oddly out of place. It had been wheeled across the paving stones to the chicken coop, the preferred collection point; by morning the tin would be gone.

The week's planting had gone well and those who had volunteered to participate were now asleep, their joints lamenting the labor. Only Father Lynch remained awake, seated by a small fire, patiently awaiting the news.

A full moon illuminated the sky and beneath its gaze the man in the field could still be seen, his white suit like a beacon. The darkness comforted him and eventually, after a time, his square shoulders turned and he looked longingly towards an unlit house. When he moved, he left a trail of broken earth.

MOTHER CULLEN was jolted awake, having heard a noise like someone urging her to be quiet. She sat up in bed and adjusted her nightgown, listening. There it was again: an entreaty in the darkness to shush. It sounded like it was coming from downstairs. Surely not Father Whittaker, who had been abed an hour or two before she had.

She threw back the covers and guided her feet into her slippers. The noise came again, this time accompanied by a thud. She felt her heart start to race and moved to the bedside cabinet, where she hastily lit the wick of a lantern. She carried it out of the room and slowly made her way down the stairs.

The noise had stopped now, but the pounding in her chest seemed louder than ever. She stepped lightly, trying not to disturb either the baby or Father Whittaker. How would she explain what she was doing? It seemed irrational. She'd probably heard a badger or a fox. How many times in the night had she awoken to such a thing? Her anxiety was nothing but a by-product of staring at the man in the field. That's what this was; a silly girl overreacting to a village tradition.

She crept towards the front door, holding the lantern high. She pulled back the bolt and opened the door. When she saw the crude white circle splashed onto the wood, she felt her body betray her and her legs gave way. She sank to the floor. She watched as thin streaks of whitewash ran between the cracks in the boards. She looked out into the starlit sky and saw another white circle mocking her, this one a flawless version of the one on the door. White moon, she thought; white circles; white suits.

Her mind cleared briefly, though her body still felt unreliable, and she carefully rose to her feet. She shuffled outside and looked up towards the front window. It was open; a white leg disappeared inside the room.

She howled, no longer caring if she woke the entire village, and dragged herself back up the stairs. She threw open the door of the front bedroom and stared at the empty crib. She ran towards the open window and allowed the moonlight to show her what she already knew: both the baby and the man in the field were gone.

CHAPTER 2

MOTHER Tanner wasn't the only one whose dreams were shattered by the noise. All along the narrow street, people were emerging from their beds, roused by Mother Cullen's howls of distress. It was a moment the entire village had been anticipating: the terrifying skirl of a woman in pain.

Mother Tanner ran down the stairs and threw open her front door. There were people already milling in the street, ominously regarded by the face of the moon. She recognized all of them, even among the shadows, and it sounded to Mother Tanner's ears like the back-fence talk had already begun.

"Who's been blessed?" Mother Fenton asked, standing in a huddle of women no more than a stone's throw from Mother Tanner's house.

"I think it's the Cullen girl," Mother Leslie said. "The door was marked as I ran past. Father Whittaker was in the street calling her name."

"All praise the Wheel!" Mother Spriggen said, closing her eyes and raising her hands to the sky.

Clot-headed fools, thought Mother Tanner as she ran past them and headed up the street. Not one of them understood the rhythms of the cycle as they claimed. They were usually too busy genuflecting before Father Lynch.

She continued her journey along the street and approached Mother Cullen's door. Father Whittaker was being consoled by half a dozen women, his silver hair bobbing with sorrow. The oak door behind him bore a dripping white circle, signifying the Turn of the Wheel. There was no room for doubt.

The man in the field had been in attendance and left his mark. All that was left was to pick up the pieces and give thanks that the sacrifice was made.

Mother Tanner looked up and down the street, filling now with more people as the news spread, many having prepared cocoa and warm bread to grace the occasion. She turned away in disgust and saw Father Lynch by the roadside, orchestrating events, earnestly coordinating a search party for the grieving Mother.

It would all be to no avail. As usual, they would aim well wide of the mark, tearing around the village like headless chickens. There was only one place Mother Cullen would have been immediately drawn to and Mother Tanner lowered her head and set off towards the darkened field where the man in the white suit had kept his silent vigil.

The cool night embraced her and she pulled her cloak about her arms and adjusted her prayer cap to cover her ears. She could still hear the fuss being made about this year's sacrifice back at Father Whittaker's house and she was glad to be away from it all. Many of the women lost all sense of decorum in such circumstances and some of the men weren't much better either. You'd think after all this time the elders of the village would be more sanguine about these events, but if anything they seemed to grow more excitable with each passing year. Father Lynch was one of the worst; his lined face nodded somberly in all the right places, but his eyes betrayed him, gleaming darkly like freshly-tilled earth.

She picked up her pace and left her gossiping neighbors behind, the noise gradually fading away. She lifted her skirts and sank her feet into the muddy field, feeling the soil clogging up the black leather of her shoes. This better be worth the effort, she thought. She could feel water leaking through the seams and turning her feet to ice. She pressed on regardless, scouring the moonlit farmland for any movement, winding across the field towards the deeper darkness of the trees.

The night was starting to feel like something from a child's nightmare, black and cold and terrifying. There was a *looseness* to it, as though time itself had slipped, plunging them all into this ready-made moment of exaltation.

There was grief, yes, but there was celebration, too, just like there had been last year, and the year before that, bringing hope for the harvest ahead.

Not that Mother Cullen would ever behold the glory of the Wheel. Mother Tanner could see her now, kneeling in the mud, her face buried in her hands as she wept. She had made the ultimate sacrifice and this was what was wrought in the aftermath: suffering and torment. Not a night would pass from this moment on where she would sleep soundly, without tears, dreaming only of feeding the chickens. Everything had changed. Night had come and brought with it the man in the field. For Mother Cullen, nothing would ever be quite the same again.

Mother Tanner approached her cautiously, arms extended to avoid a fall. It was dark here, as though even the moonlight had abandoned Mother Cullen in her moment of need, and the air was cold and unforgiving. She was only wearing her nightgown, and Mother Tanner removed her own cloak and draped it around the other woman's shoulders, at which point Mother Cullen released a choked sob that sounded like she had a mouth full of earth.

"You'll catch your death down there in the mud, dear," Mother Tanner said. "Let's get you back on your feet." She eased her hands beneath Mother Cullen's armpits and lifted her up, where she wobbled unsteadily, her body barely able to stand. Mother Tanner supported her the best she could, feeling the dreadful weight of her, as though the ordeal had drained every last ounce of energy from her bones. She felt like a sack of dirty laundry and Mother Tanner struggled to brace her against her hip.

Mother Cullen was wailing now, her head buried in her friend's shoulder, and Mother Tanner attempted to soothe her by stroking her hair and making a gentle shushing sound, like a wave breaking against the shore.

"You're all turned around right now," she said. "It's impossible to think straight. We need to get you home."

Mother Cullen tensed, her body resisting Mother Tanner's embrace. "I can't do that," she said, her voice wracked with emotion. "He has my baby. Don't you understand? *He stole him right from under my nose!*"

She broke into a fresh onslaught of uncontrolled sobbing that sounded like an old engine failing to start. It wasn't at all seemly, no matter the tragedy that had befallen her. Mother Cullen wasn't a child; she needed to pull herself together.

"Come now," Mother Tanner said. "This is getting us nowhere. Father Lynch will want to talk to you. With each Turning of the Wheel—"

"*Shut up!*" Mother Cullen spat, her eyes suddenly too wide. "I don't want to hear that shit. Not ever again. It's just something the Founding Farmers made up to turn everyone crazy. Don't you see? The whole thing is complete bullshit!"

Mother Tanner glanced over her shoulder, fearful that some of the others might have heard Mother Cullen's outburst. If Father Lynch heard such blasphemy, he'd doubtless cut out the girl's tongue.

"You shouldn't talk that way," Mother Tanner said, taking her by the shoulders and giving her a good shake. "People will hear. You want to spend half the night explaining to the Council that you misspoke?"

"Fuck the Council," Mother Cullen said. Then, turning towards the distant lights, she screamed it again: "*Fuck the Council!*"

Mother Tanner took her by the hand and roughly led her into the shadow of the trees. "You need to restrain yourself, child!" she said. "The last thing you need right now is to attract attention. You have enough to contend with."

She stared into Mother Cullen's raw eyes and held her hands. The poor girl stared back, her face swollen and glum, the fire in her belly extinguished.

"He took my child, Helen," Mother Cullen said softly. "From the crib in his room, while I was sleeping. He stole him away." She began to weep again, quietly, as though the full extent of the pain could barely be expressed. "What am I going to do?"

Mother Tanner held a cold hand to her cheek and wiped away the tears. "What they all do, I suppose. Find a way to move on."

It sounded harsh, even to Mother Tanner's own ears, but it was a message Mother Cullen needed to hear sooner rather than later. There was no value in prolonged sorrow; Father Lynch simply wouldn't allow it.

"I want to find him," Mother Cullen said, a new sense of mission compelling her. "I want to go looking for the man in the field. Has anyone ever done that before?"

Mother Tanner inhaled the cold night air and looked back towards the village. How to respond to such wide-eyed innocence? With the truth, or with a version of the truth that wouldn't leave a sour taste in her mouth? She considered the matter for a moment and then opted for the latter.

"Of course, child. It's been tried. But the man in the field is nothing and no one. You know the story as well as the rest of us. There's nothing out there."

"All I know is what they want us to know," Mother Cullen said. "He has to be somewhere. He has my baby."

She looked so distraught, Mother Tanner thought, as though someone had ripped out her heart and thrown it to the dogs. In the moonlight, Mother Cullen looked like she'd aged ten years in a matter of hours. It hardly seemed like a fair exchange for the promise of a bountiful harvest.

"We could check the woods," Mother Tanner said softly, regretting making the suggestion almost as soon as the words left her lips.

Mother Cullen nodded and rubbed at her eyes, seemingly preparing them for the search. She took control of her breathing, then took Mother Tanner's hand as they turned to face the darkened wall of trees before them. They walked carefully across the last half acre of field, squeezed between the wire fence that bordered Father Miller's land, and finally stood at the edge of the woods.

Mother Tanner glanced across at Mother Cullen and saw a woman desperately clinging to something vaguely resembling hope; whatever it was, Mother Tanner thought it looked brittle enough to crack at the slightest touch, and she turned away, feeling a deep sense of shame at having once again ignited a brightness in the woman's eyes. No matter how hard they searched, they would find nothing. It was the one unchanging variable, the only outcome set in stone. No baby had ever been recovered in Mother Tanner's long lifetime, and the man in the field remained as much a mystery now as when she'd first heard tell of him as a young girl. Not that any of that mattered right now. Mother Cullen needed a reason to go on and this was it. They would search the woods, till morning if that's what it took to convince Mother Cullen that the exercise was futile. Then Mother Tanner would do what all women in the village did on these occasions: clean up the mess and give thanks that the missing baby wasn't hers.

She followed Mother Cullen into the woods, the darkness broken only by a darting sliver of moonlight. They walked with their hands out, mindful of the strange terrain, and had covered no more than twenty meters before they were frozen by the powerful beam of a torch.

"You shouldn't be here," a man's voice said, directly in front of them. "This is private property."

Mother Tanner heard him take several steps towards them, the torch-light unwavering. She felt Mother Cullen reach out and grab hold of her arm, her breathing suddenly heavier. Like Mother Tanner, she had a hand out to shield her face from the light.

"Please lower the torch," Mother Tanner said. "It's too bright."

The man did as instructed, adjusting the beam so that it illuminated only their bodies.

"You have to go back," he said. "Mr. Lynch won't be happy that you're out here."

Mother Tanner stared at the man, her eyes slowly adjusting in the dark. Had he said *Mr* Lynch? Or had she misheard? She didn't think so. This was clearly someone from outside the village, someone who had no concept of what they were about. She looked harder at the man, trying to identify him, but the man bore no features that she recognized. Even in the shadows he looked surly, his face set into a hard, uncompromising stare. She suspected he was not a man accustomed to being opposed. Closer investigation showed a dark, unexpected shape at his hip which made Mother Tanner go cold; even to her untrained eye, there seemed little doubt that she was staring at a holstered gun.

"What are you doing here?" Mother Tanner said calmly, her curiosity eclipsing her fear. "You're blocking our path."

The man said nothing. He looked at them without moving, his eyes deep in shadow. He looked, Mother Tanner thought, like a guard, or a soldier on patrol. Is that what he was? A member of some kind of sentry unit, keeping a midnight watch over the woods? It seemed highly improbable and yet, here he was, an armed stranger, insisting they head back across the field to the village.

"This is not a place for you," he said, pointing them back the way they'd come. "You need to leave. Go back home. You will be safe there."

Mother Cullen took a step forward and Mother Tanner could see by the torchlight that she was trembling. "Please," she said, "we're looking for a man. He's wearing a white suit and carrying a baby. Have you seen him?"

The man turned his attention to Mother Cullen and shook his head. "No man. There's nothing in these woods but me. You should go home now. It's getting late."

Mother Tanner reached out a hand and drew Mother Cullen back towards her. "Let's go back," she whispered. "This doesn't feel right. Maybe someone will have more news in the village."

Mother Cullen allowed herself to be guided between the moonlit pines; Mother Tanner glanced back once over her shoulder to see the man watching them closely before he turned off his torch and disappeared into the darkness of the trees. She thought of the gun at his hip and heard him saying *Mr. Lynch won't be happy that you're out here.* It felt like she was missing something, but the two ends of the connection wouldn't meet. She tried to imagine why this area beyond the farm would need guarding in the middle of the night, but was too frazzled by the evening's events to figure it out. She strained to remember if she'd ever seen the man before; it was possible, she supposed, though it had been too dark to really get a good look at him. It was just something that happened; another thing that barely made a lick of sense on a night when wickedness had stolen across the land.

She walked back across the field behind Mother Cullen and listened to the wind and the man's voice in her head, grating and direct, telling her: *There's nothing in these woods but me.*

CHAPTER 3

FATHER Lynch sat in a rocking chair that had been hand-crafted by Father Simmons several years ago and presented to the Council during the Festival of the Autumn Equinox. A fire blazed in the hearth, heating the stone room and illuminating the faces of the three other members of the Council staring intently at Mother Tanner. They were dressed in grey linen robes worn over their everyday clothes. They looked like hawks, Mother Tanner thought, sharp-nosed and beady-eyed, coolly assessing what lay before them. She felt exposed, like a microscope specimen, and was acutely aware of the uncomfortable silence in the room.

"We'd like to thank you for speaking with us tonight," Father Lynch said at last. "We appreciate how difficult this must be."

He was the youngest of the Council members by some twenty years, though clearly had seniority over the other three. They were all aware of Council protocol and were prepared to let Father Lynch shape the conversation. His was the voice in the room to which the other three members deferred. Mother Tanner wasn't at all surprised; she had watched Father Lynch from afar for many years. He was a smooth operator, a natural communicator. When Father Lynch was around, Mother Tanner knew instinctively to lower her eyes. She tried never to give him more than was required whenever the two of them spoke.

She applied that formality now, saying nothing, just acknowledging him with a gentle bow of the head.

"It's been a long night," Father Lynch said. "A *difficult* night. Wouldn't you agree?"

Mother Tanner nodded her head. She glanced at Father Williams, the portly custodian of the village library, imagining him to be the most accommodating of the three men, but his ruddy face gave no indication that this might be the case. Father Norrick and Father Wheaks, the other two Council members, appeared equally unsympathetic, their expressions blank and unreadable. They were not here to comfort her, Mother Tanner realized, despite Father Lynch's opening remarks. They were here to cross-examine her about what she'd seen in the woods.

"Mother Cullen has been blessed," Father Lynch said, raising a glass of home-made wine to his lips. "She may not think so right now, but that will change in time. She will see what an honor it is to be visited by the man in the field."

Mother Tanner turned away, unable to look Father Lynch in the eye. The man was an idiot! Moreover, he believed implicitly in everything he said, which made him worse than an idiot; he was a zealot who had lost sight of the true path.

"You were on the scene pretty quickly," Father Lynch said. "Are you and Mother Cullen good friends?"

"Good enough," Mother Tanner said, objecting to his tone.

"I only ask because I don't recall seeing the two of you together very often."

Mother Tanner glanced at the other three men in the room, who were watching the exchange closely. She felt momentarily nauseated and wondered what would happen if she simply stood up and strode out of the room. Nothing, she thought; nothing would happen. But then she remembered the man in the woods with the holstered gun saying *Mr. Lynch won't be happy that you're out here.* She closed her eyes for a moment, trying to think, and realized she no longer knew what to believe.

"No one can see everything," she said. "You must have missed the occasions when we met."

Father Lynch chuckled and his three accomplices joined in. "I don't miss things, Mother Tanner. Not the important things. I'm aware of everything that happens in my village. That's my job."

It was a typically imperious comment, the kind that Mother Tanner had become accustomed to from Father Lynch, his lack of humility always triggering in her a profound sense of disappointment. This was the man from whom the rest of the village sought guidance; his was the voice they listened to above all others, and yet to Mother Tanner's ears the only words the man seemed to utter floated senselessly away on the same hot air in which they were produced.

"Do you understand why we've called you here tonight?" Father Williams asked, leaning forward and directing his round face in Mother Tanner's direction.

"Not really, no," she said. "I assume it's because I helped Mother Cullen in her moment of need."

Father Lynch watched her for a moment, drinking his wine, enjoying the warmth of the fire. "Yes, indeed," he said. "A touching gesture, I'm sure. What made you go down there alone?"

Mother Tanner frowned, failing to fully understand the question. "I could hear her crying. I did what I felt was right."

Father Lynch smiled briefly and gazed into the fire. "Did you ask anyone to accompany you?"

"It never occurred to me. Besides, I didn't see the need."

"Ah! A perfectly understandable reaction. You were acting instinctively. Not thinking clearly. Would that be an accurate assessment of your state of mind?"

Mother Tanner hesitated, sensing the hazards up ahead. Father Lynch had turned his attention away from the fire and was now staring at her as though the answer to the question was etched along the fine lines of her face.

"No," she said. "That would be an inaccurate assessment."

Father Lynch feigned confusion as he gazed at the other three Council members. "I see," he said. "Then perhaps you could help me out. How would you describe your state of mind?"

"I was perfectly calm. Mother Cullen was in pain. I did what I could to help her back to the village."

Father Lynch was nodding his head, his hands steepled in his lap. "And at what point did Mother Cullen suggest you go looking for the man in the field?"

Mother Tanner held herself steady, but felt a moment of pure vertigo, even though she was still sitting down. She could feel her heartbeat accelerating, her left hand trembling on the arm of the chair. How much did he know? Had someone fed him information? She tried to remember who had been first on the scene to comfort Mother Cullen when they returned, but the moment was just a blur of confused faces. She composed herself and looked at Father Lynch, unable to hold his eye for more than a second before she felt compelled to turn away.

"Every year the same thing," he went on. "Hard to imagine anything more tragic. More wine, Father Norrick?"

He leaned forward with a clay jug and poured wine into Father Norrick's empty glass, before returning his attention to Mother Tanner.

"How far did you get?" he asked.

Mother Tanner felt her skin go cold. He knows nothing, she thought. Not a thing. This is just a game; the kind a parent might play with an errant child to tease out the truth. Don't trust a single word he says.

"We walked to the edge of the woods," she said. "But it was dark and cold. I convinced Mother Cullen to turn back."

Father Lynch tipped back his head, closed his eyes and sighed. "Really," he said. "You weren't tempted to go further? You didn't feel an obligation to take poor Mother Cullen beyond the fence?"

"I was afraid of getting lost."

"Goodness, yes! That would make sense. The wood is no place to be on a night such as this."

Father Wheaks, no more than a spectator up to this point, coughed into his hand and said, "Did you see anyone out there? Past the field?"

Mother Tanner noticed that Father Lynch shot him an annoyed glance and she felt a flicker of satisfaction. The man with the holstered gun surfaced in her mind again, but she had no intention of mentioning him to any of the Council members. He would remain a secret. The less Father Lynch and his cronies knew, the better; that way, she would always have the edge. She would consider the implications of the man in the woods in her own time. Her instinct was to give Father Lynch only what he already knew.

She turned to Father Wheaks and innocently asked, "Who would I have seen?"

Father Lynch flapped his hand towards Father Wheaks, largely to shut him up, Mother Tanner suspected, and then summoned one of his insincere smiles. "I think we're all curious about the man in the field. Even those of us who should know better." He glared again at Father Wheaks, who sat back in his chair and buried his face in his glass of home-made wine.

"Such a strange night," Father Lynch went on. "So many mixed emotions. It's easy to get confused with so much going on."

Mother Tanner said nothing, remembering her own golden rule: no question, no response.

Father Lynch smiled, presumably well aware of the strategy. She could almost see the cogs working inside his head, mirroring the great Turning of the Wheel, the complexity of memory and time conjoined, as though life itself conformed solely to the disposition of Father Lynch.

"I wonder," he said, "did you find what you were looking for?" His eyes were watching her with frightening intensity, daring her to look away.

"We found each other," Mother Tanner said softly.

There was a slight pause, before Father Lynch said, "We're all grateful for that, at least."

His expression suggested that this sentiment couldn't have been further from the truth. He knew he had just been fed a line, something that sounded dangerously like a rallying cry for Mothers everywhere, and he didn't like it in the slightest. Mother Tanner, though she might not be aware of it herself, was a menace, a genuine threat to the well-being of the village. He had been watching her closely for a number of years. She was quietly respectful, reserved, aloof. He had been unable to charm his way into her heart, like he had with so many of the other women. Her resistance was cool and unyielding. Mother Tanner was a woman who led her life according to an unseen schematic locked away inside her head. It would take more than Father Lynch's oily inducements for her to ever see him as anything other than a fraud.

"You've been with the village a long time," he said. "Longer than I can recall. Do you find our community to your liking?"

"It is the life we chose," Mother Tanner replied. "My husband and I."

"Ah, yes! Our beloved servant Harold. We all remember him fondly." He looked to the other three Council members, who were nodding in agreement. "A gifted carpenter, if I remember correctly."

Mother Tanner bowed her head, not wanting to think of her late husband while looking into the furtive eyes of Father Lynch.

"Sadly, not everyone feels the same way as you and I, Mother Tanner. There are people in the village who would question our faith. Our culture is not for everyone, after all."

He gazed pointedly at Mother Tanner, who allowed the silence to grow, more comfortable with the dead air than with Father Lynch's disclosure.

"Perhaps you know of one or two people yourself who are discontented," Father Williams said. "People who might benefit from a little education..."

Mother Tanner didn't like the sound of that; she looked at each of them before saying, "I know of no such person."

Father Lynch scratched his temple and allowed the silence to drift. "Those who help enrich the lives of our extended family are always well received by this committee. It would be helpful to us if you could use your influence in the village to advocate on behalf of the Council."

Mother Tanner thought the matter through for all of five seconds before nodding graciously and saying, "Of course. I'll do what I can." Any answer other than this would have put Father Lynch and his confederates on high alert. This she could do without; she already suspected she would be on the Council's radar in the immediate future. The easy answer—the *prudent* answer—was the one she gave. She sensed intuitively that this was what Father Lynch had been working towards all along.

He smiled, his teeth darkened by wine, and rose to dismiss her. "The Council thanks you," he said.

CHAPTER 4

MOTHER Tanner left the conference chamber and walked directly to Mother Saunders' house. It was still pitch black and she was guided only by the occasional gas lamp hanging in a number of the nearby porches. It was cold too, and she hurried along, keen to be inside by a warm fire. The conversation with Father Lynch and his three acolytes—Council members in name only, it would seem—had unsettled her and she felt drained from having to withstand the piercing gaze of Father Lynch. Being at the center of his world for such a sustained period of time had left her feeling dirty. All she wanted now was to sit by a roaring fire with a hot cocoa in her hand. Mother Saunders would take care of that, just as she'd agreed to take in Mother Cullen. Those still gathered at the house could provide Mother Tanner with a full update on the girl's condition. She hoped they'd had the good sense to add a sedative to Mother Cullen's tea; without it, she feared the girl would be lying awake replaying the night's horrors on an endless loop.

She arrived at the house and knocked gently on the door. It was opened by Mother Gilmore who took her by the arm and ushered her in from the cold.

"Lord, you must be frozen half to death," she said. "Where the devil have you been?"

Mother Tanner entered the house and felt the heat stinging her cheeks. She removed her cloak and hung it in the hall, next to the others. "I was summoned by the Council. Father Lynch wanted to convey his concern."

Mother Gilmore rolled her eyes. "He's all heart."

Mother Tanner smiled and walked through to the front room. There was, indeed, a fire blazing in the hearth, just as Mother Tanner had hoped. There were also a number of women watching her enter the room, visibly exhausted by having spent the early hours of the morning tending to Mother Cullen. Mother Tanner was pleased to see that the girl herself was not present, for which she was immensely grateful. She didn't think she had the energy to offer any more comfort tonight; her resources were utterly depleted.

She nodded at the ladies huddled either side of the fire, pleased to see Mother Saunders again, her hand resting protectively on the knee of her sixteen-year-old daughter, Alice. Standing behind them was Mother Glatt, a large imposing woman with arms like fence posts, accustomed to doing the work of two men when necessary and usually in half the time. On the other side of the hearth sat Mother Belfield, a plump woman with a face like a squeezed-out dish rag. Mother Tanner felt herself go tense at the sight of her. She felt naturally disinclined to talk whenever Mother Belfield was around. The woman was an unknown quantity, as far as Mother Tanner was concerned. She was never entirely sure that Mother Belfield had anyone's interests at heart but her own; when she spoke, it often sounded as though her words were coated with a toxin that only Mother Tanner was able to detect.

"How is she?" she asked, instinctively turning to Mother Saunders and seating herself in the last available armchair.

"I can't imagine she's ever felt worse," Mother Saunders said. "Poor mite. She looks dreadful. Like her body's already given up the fight."

"It's to be expected," Mother Gilmore said, reaching for a biscuit. "If it had ever been my Billy..." She trailed off and Mother Saunders broke the silence by tapping Alice on the shoulder. "Run along now," she said. "Make Helen a nice mug of hot cocoa. She deserves it more than any of us."

Alice departed to make Mother Tanner's drink and could be heard rattling around in the adjacent kitchen. Mother Belfield's scrunched up face turned towards Mother Tanner and seemed to be listening for something, her cheeks burned red by the flames.

"I can't imagine they're very happy," she said.

They all knew to whom she was referring and waited quietly for Mother Tanner to reply.

"Why's that, Margaret?"

Mother Belfield sniffed. "You and Ruth were in the field. Rumor has it you went into the woods. The Council is very strict about that. Father Lynch has delivered sermons about it."

"No one went into the woods," Mother Tanner said. "And the Council was very understanding. More so than I expected, actually."

Mother Saunders smiled and reached over and took Mother Tanner by the hand. "That's good then," she said. "Them being so reasonable. We were all a bit worried."

Mother Tanner smiled back, doubting whether Mother Saunders was speaking on behalf of the whole group. Mother Belfield was watching her closely; Mother Tanner didn't have to try too hard to imagine the look on the woman's face if the Council had prescribed a formal punishment. She would have been front and center, wearing a clean smock and prayer cap, waiting for the fun to begin.

Alice returned and handed Mother Tanner a steaming mug of cocoa. She wrapped her hands around it, grateful for the warmth spreading through her palms.

"Thank you," she said. "I needed this."

Alice nodded and returned to her place by Mother Saunders.

"What happened to Father Whittaker? He looked in quite a state when I last saw him."

Mother Tanner noticed the other women glance at one another before Mother Belfield said, "He was next in with the Council after you. He was in the house with her, after all." She turned up her nose as though she'd just detected a bad smell. "That arrangement never did sit right. Too cozy by far."

Mother Tanner held her face above the heat of the cocoa for a moment, watching Mother Belfield over the top of the mug. "What are you suggesting?"

Mother Belfield held Mother Tanner's gaze for a moment before turning away. "Nothing, I'm sure," she said. "Not in present company anyway."

Before Mother Tanner could press her further, Mother Saunders rose from her chair and moved to the center of the room. "This is uncalled for. Let's focus on poor Ruth. She's the one we need to be thinking of right now. Everything else is just an unwelcome distraction." She looked pointedly at Mother Belfield as she spoke and refused to look away until Mother Belfield finally lowered her eyes.

"Has she been sedated?" Mother Tanner asked.

"I put a few herbs in her tea," Mother Saunders said. "She should sleep right through. There's no telling what she might encounter in her dreams, though. Nothing good, I'm sure."

She fussed around the room gathering the empty mugs and disappeared into the kitchen. The room fell silent for a while and when Mother Saunders returned she was carrying a plate of toasted bread and cheese.

"Dig in," she said. "The bread's fresh today."

They all helped themselves, Mother Tanner relishing the simple combination of buttered bread and melted cheddar, having neglected to eat for much of the day. She noticed that all the women in the room were looking tired, events having exacted a heavy toll on all of them, and they had clearly reached a point where it was easier to eat than to talk.

After a while, though, the silence grew uncomfortable and Mother Gilmore, often the one most inclined to rake over old coals, leaned forward in her chair.

"It's the same every year," she said. "One of us has to give up what we love most. It wouldn't work otherwise."

Mother Glatt made a noise deep in the back of her throat. "Horseshit! That's exactly what they want us to think—"

Mother Tanner, seeing that Mother Belfield was watching Mother Glatt intently, cut her off. "Maybe this conversation can wait for another day," she said. "There's no value to be had in treading the same old ground. There are other things to concern ourselves with. Like the Offering..."

The other women said nothing for a moment, their thoughts suddenly turning to the celebration that awaited Mother Cullen the following day.

"It should be regarded as a blessing," Mother Belfield said. "Just as the Council intended. It's a great honor, after all."

"Perhaps that's the best way to look at it," Mother Gilmore said. "Like a gift."

Mother Saunders sighed heavily. "It's not a gift, Susan. It's just horrible and you know it. Stop pretending you think otherwise. It's not at all seemly."

Mother Gilmore bristled, her cheeks turning bright red. "I was simply looking for a break in the clouds, Hilda. The day's been dark enough as it is, don't you think?"

"Absolutely. But let's speak plainly, shall we? Otherwise we'll lose all sense of perspective."

Mother Tanner was inclined to agree with this sentiment, but kept her counsel, more disposed to sit back and watch how the others framed the debate.

She wasn't at all surprised when Mother Glatt, never one to stand on ceremony, placed her large forearms on the back of Mother Saunders' chair and said, "I'll speak plainly enough for all of us. The Offering is a man's solution to a problem created by men. It's obscene."

"Ask Mother Lowton or Mother Nyland if they agree with you," Mother Belfield said. "I daresay they'd have quite a different opinion. Leanne has gone on record as saying that the Offering was the saving grace of her life."

Mother Glatt seemed to brood in the glow of the fire. "Going on record does not necessarily mean Mother Nyland spoke true. The two are far from the same thing."

"I agree," Mother Saunders said. "Sometimes it's easier to say what you know they want to hear. I've done it myself."

Mother Tanner interjected at this point, keen to erase the shine from Mother Belfield's eyes. "Doubtless we've all done it at some point. Even you, Margaret. Isn't that so?"

Mother Belfield lowered her eyes. "A time or two, perhaps. Just to flatten out one or two bumps in the road."

"Exactly. That's why we all do it," Mother Tanner said, smiling. "For road repairs."

The women laughed and the tension that had been steadily building as the night dragged on quickly dissolved.

"I suggest at this point that we take our leave of Hilda and Alice and work in shifts here at the house just in case Ruth's sedative wears off. I'll take the first hour, then Margaret can relieve me, followed by Susan and Gertrude."

"I'll put up a cot in Alice's room," Mother Saunders said, making for the stairs.

"The armchair will be just fine," Mother Tanner said. "I doubt any of us will be getting much sleep tonight anyway. Too much white noise."

The women rose as one, tidied away the plates, and said their goodbyes, before those that were leaving slowly filed out of the house.

CHAPTER 5

THE next morning Mother Tanner awoke to a loud knocking on her front door. She felt disoriented and couldn't remember how she had made her way back to her own house, though at some point she had clearly stumbled home in the early hours and instantly fallen asleep in her own bed. Now, with her mind still fuzzy with yesterday's traumas, she glanced at the clock on her bedside table and saw that she had been more exhausted than she thought. It was 9:25 AM, more than three hours past the time she normally rose, and she rubbed at her face, as though doing so might restore some degree of awareness in her otherwise addled mind. She straightened her fringe and kicked back the sheets, inviting in the cold morning air. Her memory of an uncomfortable hour's sleep in Mother Saunders' armchair came flooding back and she felt the ache of it at the base of her spine. There was another knock at the door, louder this time, and she rearranged her nightgown, muttering something under her breath. She pulled on her robe and walked to the window. When she opened it and looked out, she saw Father Miller's son, Michael, standing on the doorstep heating his hands with his breath.

"This had better be important!" she shouted down. "I'm not in the best of moods."

Michael looked up at the woman peering from the window. "Message from Father Lynch," he said. "There's to be—"

"For the love of God, boy, don't shout it to the world! Wait till I come down."

She closed the window, still feeling far from hospitable, and made her way downstairs to the front door. She opened it on to a red-faced young man who was hopping from foot to foot to keep warm.

"What is it, child? And if you tell me something disagreeable, like as not you'll soon have an ear the same color as your chops!"

Michael hesitated, uncertain whether he should go on, until Mother Tanner sighed and gave him an encouraging nod.

"Father Lynch wants everyone to be at the main square in thirty minutes. He's preparing the Offering. He especially wanted you to be there, Mother Tanner. He made me swear that yours was the first house I called on."

"Did he now?" Mother Tanner said. "How…thoughtful of him."

Michael smiled broadly, as though he had been patted on the head. "Can I give word of your attendance?"

Mother Tanner glanced out across the fields beyond the lane leading to her house, thinking of poor Mother Cullen. "I'm sure that'll be fine, Michael," she said. "Tell Father Lynch and the rest of the Council I'll be somewhere in the crowd, watching carefully. You might also take a moment to remind him that the judgement of the good Lord shall descend upon those present foolish enough to take the land, or anyone on it, for granted."

Michael stared at her curiously, then nodded his head, smiled and moved along.

THERE WAS still a chill in the air by the time Mother Tanner made her way down the lane and across the yard to the main square. She pulled her cloak tightly around her shoulders and eased herself into the crowd, nodding politely at those she had reason to mistrust and smiling at others for whom she did not. Although the people gathered in the square were essentially the same as those assembled in Father Miller's yard yesterday, the mood was noticeably different. There were a few engaged in quiet conversation, but for the most part, the square was silent, no matter that the Council insisted that the Offering was a great celebration of life, confirmation of the Turning of the Wheel and the bounty it sometimes chose to bestow.

Not so for Mother Tanner, nor for many of the others waiting in the square who had borne witness to this ceremony before. The Offering was a time to reflect on the legacy of the man in the field; to consider what had been taken and renounce the suffering left in his wake.

Hard to imagine how their future could be shaped any other way; at least, as far as Father Lynch was concerned. For Mother Tanner, the road forward was always more complex than sacrificing blood for bounty, but she knew her place in the grand scheme of things. They all did. That's what made the Turning of the Wheel so relevant, she supposed. Ultimately, it drove on regardless, disdainful of whatever lay in its path.

She lowered her head and worked her way in among the crowd, until eventually she pulled up alongside Mother Saunders, Alice and Mother Glatt. They looked tired and drawn and Mother Tanner guessed her own face was equally pale, the night having wrung from her weary bones what little energy she had left.

"Quite a night," Mother Saunders said, her voice barely audible for fear of being overheard.

Mother Tanner pulled her prayer cap down so that it covered much of her face and allowed her eyes to scan the crowd. "And the grief only just begun, I'm sure. I keep thinking about Ruth and try to imagine how she must be feeling."

"Who knows," Mother Saunders said. "Maybe she'll accept the Offering and be redeemed."

Mother Glatt looked disgusted even at the thought of such a thing. "You've spent too many years tuned in to Father Lynch," she said. "Listen to him for too long and he'll have you believing you piss blood and bleed water."

Mother Tanner ignored Mother Glatt's comment, though she thought much of what she'd said—while a trifle crude—a more than accurate depiction of how Father Lynch held court.

"Where's Ruth now?" she said. "Does anybody know?"

Mother Saunders shook her head. "They came for her early this morning and took her away. My guess is she's being prepared in Father Miller's barn."

"Did you get a chance to speak with her? To talk her through the process?"

Another shake of the head from Mother Saunders. "We weren't thinking clearly. We wanted to let her rest. By the time it had occurred to any of us, it was too late."

It was understandable, Mother Tanner thought; she would probably have done the same thing. Yet what she would give to have just five minutes alone with Mother Cullen before this damn ceremony began, just to remind her of what was to come. The ritual of rebirth was no less complicated than any other planting; no less messy, either. It was often more traumatic than the sacrifice that had preceded it and had brought many women to their knees, broken and forlorn, as the Wheel slowly turned and crushed what was left of their lives.

"Good morning, ladies," a voice said, intruding on Mother Tanner's somber preoccupation. She glanced up and saw Mother Belfield's puckered face, the woman having stolen up on them without their noticing. "Another glorious day!"

Mother Glatt grunted. "It's cold and my nipples ache," she said.

"Well, I've got a stiff neck," Mother Belfield replied, grinning, "but I'm not going to brag about it!"

There was a short, uncomfortable silence as Mother Belfield eased between Alice and Mother Glatt, forcing herself into the huddle they had formed.

"You seem unusually happy today, Margaret," Mother Tanner said. "You find an extra penny in your purse?"

Mother Belfield smiled. "Even better. I woke up this morning and remembered it was the day of the Offering. Hard to imagine that it only comes around once a year."

Alice, normally so intense and timid, looked at Mother Belfield and said, "That might be me up there one day. The man in the field might choose me."

"Then you'll be blessed, child, like Mother Cullen will be today. The whole community will give thanks and celebrate in your name."

"But what about my baby?" Alice said, looking around at the older women.

Mother Belfield placed a hand on her shoulder and smiled again. "In time it will be forgotten. You'll accept the Offering and move on with your life, like others before you. And the whole village will be eternally grateful for the harvest you secure. Trust me, no one will be more proud than Father Lynch."

Perfectly on cue—as though saying his name acted as a kind of esoteric summons—Father Lynch stepped onto the raised platform at the front of the crowd and raised his hands.

"After the reaping," he said, his impressive voice filling the square, "the sowing of the seed. This is the cycle we complete, a communion of fertility and transformation, stimulating a natural cleansing of the land. Balance, my friends. That is how we survive. A spiritual reawakening is ours if we simply reach out and accept that we and the soil are one."

There was a smattering of applause, but it felt like a moment missed as the crowd tried to establish their place in the ceremony. Never one to be easily discouraged, Father Lynch smiled serenely and pressed on.

"The Offering is upon us. A gift from our community to she who has sacrificed the most. *Behold,* the Book of Psalms tells us, *children are a heritage from the LORD, the fruit of the womb a reward.* And so we bow our heads and give thanks to Mother Cullen for her beneficence, balancing the weight of the Wheel and bringing us here to this square. Look around you, friends, see how our family gathers to repay Mother Cullen's kindness, how we congregate to settle the debts of Mother Earth and bring into alignment a true fellowship for the harvest ahead."

Mother Tanner turned her head to one side, barely able to listen to any more of Father Lynch's rhetoric. Besides, she'd heard it all before and while the language might change, the sentiment did not. It was powerful stuff, no doubt about it, but she remained skeptical of its author, for whom bloated oration and an insincere smile—his currency of choice—came easily, every word as smooth as a cheap seduction.

She watched the crowd and was unsurprised to see nearly every face fixed on Father Lynch, eyes glazed with reverence. Every polished word that tumbled from his mouth caught the ear of its audience and worked its magic, the message irrelevant, the crowd responding to the simple harmony of his voice.

"Let us each pause for a moment of reflection," Father Lynch went on, "to consider the trials of our beloved Mother Cullen, without whom our crops would be blighted, our rejoicing much reduced." His right arm extended, as though he were introducing a trapeze artist, and Mother Cullen was led onto the platform from a crumbling farm building at the back of the square. She was accompanied by Father Miller, who was supporting her by the arm, trying to disguise the fact that, had he not been doing so, there was every chance the girl would simply have collapsed onto the rough cobbles of the yard.

Mother Tanner paled at the sight of Mother Cullen. In little more than twelve hours, she had gone from being a vibrant young girl to an old woman, haggard and ashen-faced, every second of the previous night's misery etched into her sallow features. The Council had dressed her in a billowing white robe, presumably to facilitate the Offering, and Mother Tanner had to hold herself steady so as not to convey her disgust.

"*Do not hold back offerings from your granaries or your vats,* the Lord tells us. *You must give me the firstborn of your sons.* We stand here today to bear testimony to the will of the Lord and implore each one of you to give your blessing upon this day so that Mother Cullen may be filled with your love."

Father Lynch looked out among the crowd, his eyes roving over every face assembled in the square, seemingly making a mental note of any absentee. Mother Tanner wondered what the price might be for failing to attend the ceremony. It didn't bear thinking about. She pictured the man in the woods with the holstered gun and felt a chill run down her spine. *Mr. Lynch won't be happy*, he had said. Mother Tanner glanced at the crowd again and felt a heaviness in her heart. They all knew it; they just didn't talk about it; it didn't do to upset Father Lynch.

"We make the Offering in the Lord's name," he said, "always seeking to replace what was lost, to rebuild what was destroyed, to fertilize what the innocent have sown. This young woman—" He pointed to Mother Cullen who stood with her head swaying, rocking awkwardly against Father Miller's support; her eyes looked cloudy and unfocused and Mother Tanner wondered what medication the Council had forced upon her to see her through the toughest part of the day. "—knows what true pain feels like. But today, with the Lord's blessing, she will begin the long process of healing."

Father Lynch fell silent and gazed out across the crowd until his eyes fell on Mother Tanner. He smiled like a man who has just been awarded a prize.

"Mother Tanner, why don't you join us on the platform? After all, yours is the voice that Mother Cullen first heard when she was down in the field. Perhaps you could lead us all in prayer as she takes her first steps on the road to recovery..."

There was a moment of silence as heads began to turn in Mother Tanner's direction; then Mother Belfield began to applaud, her face beaming with misplaced pride, encouraging others to slowly join in, until Mother Tanner had little choice but to make her way towards the front of the square.

"That's the spirit!" Father Lynch said. "The Lord tells us *He who walks with the wise grows wise*, and there are none wiser in our humble community than Mother Tanner!"

The applause was louder now as Father Lynch cranked up the rhetoric, watching Mother Tanner carefully as she approached the platform. She glanced at Mother Cullen, trying to make eye contact, but up close it was obvious that the girl had been more liberally drugged than she had first thought. She fought to remain calm and stared at Father Miller, her eyes searching his face for any sign of remorse, prompting him to look away, unable to hold her gaze for more than a few seconds.

She walked along the platform until she was standing beside Father Lynch. She could feel her hands trembling and she thought she could hear the echo of her own heartbeat in her head. She turned to face the crowd and made every effort to contain her emotion, knowing that anything less would only further gratify Father Lynch. She looked out at people she had known all her life and tried to imagine how their dream of an idyllic community had brought them to this moment, staring up at a man whose faith was at best questionable, waiting for a young girl to lose another part of herself in a ceremony they only partly understood. The Offering was an attempt at redressing the balance, but twisted into something terrible, until it looked to Mother Tanner like a deformed parody of itself, an appalling heresy dressed up as an invocation of the Lord. She suddenly wanted no part of it, yet there was nothing she could do but keep her eyes firmly fixed on Father Lynch and wait for the horror to descend.

It began sooner than she thought. Father Lynch ushered her to one side—none too gently, as it happened—and smiled out at the crowd.

"This year's Offering," he said, "will be made by Father Cawson's son, David, a young man of great integrity who was personally selected by the Council earlier in the day."

His arm extended again like a circus barker inviting in the clowns, and David Cawson appeared from the same dilapidated building at the back of the square from which Mother Cullen had first emerged. He looked nervous, his smile awkward and his eyes anxiously surveying the crowd. A low murmur could be heard among those watching, though what this might represent Mother Tanner had no idea. She too looked across at David and was surprised by how big the boy had grown, his body lean and muscular, his arms powerful from working the fields and helping Father Cawson with the livestock. How old was he now? Nineteen? Maybe twenty? Certainly no older than that; he still had the look of an innocent about him, which would, of course, have made him all the more suitable to perform the duty required of him by the Council.

He walked towards Father Lynch with his shoulders hunched, his eyes moving quickly from Mother Cullen to the crowd. He looked like a startled mouse, albeit one that had stolen into the larder and gorged endlessly on the provisions inside. Mother Tanner had thought the boy an imbecile when he was growing up and had no reason to doubt that assessment now. He was the perfect man for the job: young, strong as an ox and just as easily led. The kind of vessel Father Lynch would have been instinctively drawn to for the Offering.

She watched with a kind of cold horror working its way through her body as Father Lynch took David by the arm and guided him to within striking distance of Mother Cullen.

"We make this Offering," he said, "to wash away the pain; to ease the suffering that attends our darkest moments." He positioned both himself and David so that the crowd had a clear view of proceedings; Father Miller did the same with Mother Cullen, bracing her against his hip and placing the palm of his hand against her back.

"It is for you, Mother Cullen, to decide: do you accept our Offering?"

There was a long moment of silence in which Mother Tanner thought she could hear the relentless Turning of the Wheel. Father Lynch watched and waited, suddenly looking anxious. He glanced at Father Miller who simply stood firm, uncertain how he was expected to respond. Mother Cullen, washed out and barely functioning, just stared into space, presumably still inwardly searching for her missing child, her eyes dulled by narcotics and the empty hours of confronting the future alone.

"Take your time, child," Father Lynch said, smiling out at the crowd to reassure them that all was well. "You are surrounded by your family. Everyone here is with you."

Another moment of silence passed. Mother Tanner held her breath, praying for Mother Cullen to give the one answer that would send shockwaves racing through the crowd and turn the Council to stone.

"I ask again," Father Lynch said, louder this time. "Do you accept our Offering?"

The words finally seemed to trigger something in Mother Cullen and her eyes widened, just for a fraction of a second, as she leaned forward, stared into the eyes of David Cawson, and said, "I do."

Mother Tanner visibly slumped, her whole body feeling hollow. She wondered what enchantment Father Lynch had worked—what oily sermon he must have preached—to force Mother Cullen to cooperate. It had to be something unnatural; some glamour, perhaps, over which only Father Lynch could claim control. That was it, surely.

She blinked and in that moment tried to imagine what it must be like to be Father Lynch, an instrument of God, wielding the breathtaking power bestowed upon him by his own people. She desperately wanted to believe that Mother Cullen wouldn't have accepted the Offering without some kind of outside intervention, but why would she think such a thing? She only knew Mother Cullen as a passing acquaintance. A nod of the head, a smile in the street, a polite word or two in Mother Teggard's grocery store. That was the extent of it. Did she really know the woman well enough to make any sort of judgement beyond that? She wanted to blame Father Lynch for Mother Cullen's lame acceptance of the Offering, but in truth those two terrible words were of her own making. *I do* Mother Cullen had said; and that was all that was needed for the time-honored ceremony to begin.

Father Lynch raised his arms above his head and urged David to step forward.

"Then let the Wheel turn and the Offering commence!" he said.

Father Miller transferred the quivering bundle that was Mother Cullen into the arms of David Cawson and the two were shepherded off the platform and back into the old farm building behind them. The crowd applauded as they left, much to Mother Tanner's dismay, and she stood alone on the platform, feeling somehow complicit, as though the whole service had been conducted with her tacit approval.

"As the Lord decreed," Father Lynch said, his voice detonating like a bomb around the square, "our Offering has been accepted! *One person gives freely, yet gains even more.* This is the truth as proclaimed by the Lord. And now Mother Cullen, our glorious witness, will receive after giving, shall be blessed after feeling totally alone. Let the Lord give back what the man in the field took away! Oh, Holy Creator, we implore you to enrich our sister with your love!"

Father Lynch turned to Mother Tanner at this point, his expression stern and uncompromising, urging her to begin the prayer as David and Mother Cullen disappeared inside the dimly-lit building.

Mother Tanner felt a flush of panic and stared out at the expectant crowd. Her mind had completely emptied of anything remotely appropriate and she found herself breathing heavily, her thoughts muddled and confused, waiting like everyone else for the screams.

"Mother Tanner, a prayer, if you would?" Father Lynch's expression had darkened and she could see the rage simmering behind his eyes.

She nodded and hesitantly began, her words barely audible. "The Lord brings death and makes alive; he brings down to the grave and raises up. The Lord sends poverty and wealth; he humbles and he exalts..."

From the farm building behind the platform, the first screams rang out across the square. Mother Cullen sounded like she was putting up a fight, Mother Tanner thought. Good for her.

She looked down at the crowd and saw that many were leaving, especially those with young children whose ears would fail to understand the message of consecration in Mother Cullen's defiant roar.

"He raises the poor from the dust," Mother Tanner went on, "and lifts the needy from the ash heap; he seats them with princes and has them inherit a throne of honor. For the foundations of the earth are the Lord's; on them he has set the world. He will guard the feet of his faithful servants, but the wicked will be silenced in the place of darkness. Amen."

Mother Tanner closed her eyes. The screams continued. She ran through a silent prayer of her own, her hands clasped tightly together, the weight of the moment immense. Soon the Offering would be over; there was that, at least. It was all she could hold onto: that the ceremony would eventually end. The seed would be planted, the Wheel would turn and the cycle would be newly begun.

CHAPTER 6

It felt wrong to be making lunch after what she'd just witnessed, but it was the only activity in which Mother Tanner could find comfort; and so she baked bread, sliced ham and prepared a plate of cheese and pickle on the side.

She paused in her work and stared out of the kitchen window at the ploughed fields stretching towards the woodland beyond. A dark sea of rolling mud swept right up to a line of trees on the horizon. This was their life, and always had been. The rich soil; the tilled earth; a continuous renewal of the land. Today, though, it felt tainted. All of it, the idyllic setting spoiled rotten to the core. She closed her eyes and took long, rejuvenating breaths, trying to cleanse her soul of any lingering impurity, Mother Cullen's screams still ringing in her head.

A dark day, she thought; a terrible day. Another horrifying example of men seeing themselves as the solution instead of the problem; the cold hand of the Council pressing down on the village, urging everyone to pray hard and rejoice. She asked herself again why she stayed, why she endured the rituals and ceremonies of Father Lynch, and knew that the answer lay rooted in the distorted shadow of her childhood. This was how she'd been raised; it was how they were all raised. What was part of you stayed part of you, no matter how complicated. Turning away from it did not necessarily mean that you left the sorrow behind; it just meant you couldn't see it coming, which to Mother Tanner was the worst of all roads.

She shook the thought from her head and focused not on the past but on the immediate task of cleaning up the kitchen, returning each item to the cool interior of the pantry. The darkened space felt immeasurably better than the brightness of the day, which served only to remind her of the things she no longer wanted to see. She paused a while, resting her head on one of the shelves. It felt good, a strange form of therapy, the smells of pastries and preserves momentarily lifting her spirits. After a while, though, as was perhaps inevitable, the relief drained away. She felt mildly embarrassed. Hiding in the pantry, she thought; such a juvenile response. Hadn't she done exactly the same thing when she was a young girl, searching for a private hideaway during planting season? How depressing to think that life could be such a hollow cycle of behavior, each action an echo of some earlier circumstance that time would eventually grind into dust. She held onto the thought for no more than was long enough to feel jarred into action before she braced herself and emerged into the light.

What she had seen today—what Mother Cullen had been forced to endure—was like something from a nightmare. Deep down she knew this to be the case; the horror of it was palpable. Yet she knew also that these rituals—these flawed, complex solemnities—were part of who they were. That was the truth of the matter. Whether this was enough to legitimize the Council's more esoteric customs was another matter entirely; a question for another day and a wiser head than hers.

Besides, she'd been deliberating on this issue for as long as she could remember and had never found herself on the right side of the argument. That she was conflicted was only part of the problem. What always stung her into a profound sense of sadness was that, no matter how much she was appalled by the Offering—and it never failed to leave a mark on her soul—there was a part of her that embraced the formality of it. This was the issue that burned when she considered it for too long, as was her present compulsion. She could never explain how she truly felt; indeed, it occurred to her that it might even be futile to try. It made her feel ill when she dwelt on it for too long. Her impulse was to put it to one side, as she felt determined to do now, no matter how insistently it played on her mind.

Allowing the matter to recede into the darkness became notably easier when she saw Mother Saunders walking up the path towards the front door. Mother Tanner breathed a sigh of relief and wiped her hands on the towel hanging by the sink. A little company was just what the doctor ordered. She had been alone long enough; any longer and her rational mind might just have found a way to betray what little of her faith remained.

She opened the door before Mother Saunders had the chance to knock and welcomed her inside. She was alone this time, having left Alice at home. This in itself was uncommon. The pair went everywhere together, mother and daughter well known within the community as inseparable companions: where one went, so too the other. Not, however, on this occasion.

"No Alice?" Mother Tanner asked, hanging Mother Saunders' cloak by the door.

"She's with Ronald painting the back fence. She's seen and heard enough. I forget sometimes that she's still a child."

Mother Tanner smiled. Alice was a young woman and a level-headed one at that, yet Mother Saunders refused to see her as anything other than her sweet little girl. Perhaps this was true of all parents, she thought. Releasing a child into the world must be terrifying. So many hidden dangers; so many ways a child can be deceived by the wicked, losing their way along the path.

It was another bleak thought, one of many this morning, and Mother Tanner promptly erased it and ushered Mother Saunders into the kitchen.

"Coffee?"

"Lovely." Mother Saunders lowered herself into a chair and stared at the spread laid out on the table. "You expecting company, Helen?"

"No," Mother Tanner said. "Just hopeful." She smiled and felt the weight of the day in the effort. "You arrived right on cue. Please, help yourself. The cheese is Father Willett's aged cheddar."

Mother Saunders pulled up two plates while Mother Tanner attended to the coffee. She cut up the bread and sliced the cheese, nibbling at the pickles as she worked. Mother Tanner brought over the coffees and joined her at the table.

"Any word on Ruth?" she asked. "The Offering usually exacts quite a heavy toll. Do we know where she was taken after the…" Mother Tanner scrabbled around for a sensitive way to end the sentence she'd begun, but then merely left it hanging in the air, the words, whatever they might have been, unspoken.

The two women sipped at their coffee, neither looking the other in the eye.

"That's really why I'm here," Mother Saunders said. "Ruth was taken to the Council chambers—to rejoice in the glory, apparently." Though she sounded disgusted, Mother Tanner thought the woman simply looked tired and resigned. "I'm guessing Father Lynch just wanted to keep a close eye on her. Not that he did a very good job. Ruth got out anyway and now nobody knows where she is."

Mother Tanner froze, her mug caught halfway between the table and her mouth. Hard though it was to believe, the day was not yet done emptying its sorrow into the earth.

"Have they checked with Father Whittaker? She could be hiding in the house."

Mother Saunders was shaking her head. "Father Miller and his boys have already searched it. She isn't there."

"Well, where else is there? She has to be somewhere."

Mother Saunders looked around the kitchen, appearing flustered and ashamed. "I was hoping she might have come here. You and Ruth seemed to have formed some kind of connection, Helen. In the best of all worlds, she'd be here in your house, drinking cocoa and listening to the radio."

Mother Tanner's expression darkened and she slowly placed her mug on the table, never once taking her eyes off Mother Saunders. "You mentioned this to Father Lynch, I suppose, and the damn Council!"

Mother Saunders looked offended, though she lowered her eyes, clearly having briefly considered doing so. "Of course not!" she said. "If I had, they'd be here right now instead of me. You know that."

This was true, though it still left Mother Tanner with a sour taste in her mouth. Had she reached the point where she no longer trusted anyone, not even Mother Saunders? She took a deep breath, searching for a more composed approach to the problem; getting angry with those closest to her would hardly improve matters.

"If Ruth had reached out to you I thought I might be able to help. That's why I told Alice to stay at home. I hoped I might be a more welcome sight than Father Lynch."

Mother Tanner sighed and closed her fingers around Mother Saunders' hand. "Oh, Hilda, you are. Of course you are. I just…this whole thing has got under my skin more than I imagined. I'm a little on edge."

Mother Saunders smiled and patted Mother Tanner's hand. "We all are," she said. "That's what they count on, I suppose. Us turning on each other. Betraying our friends to the Council. It's how they've operated for years."

"Doesn't that concern you? That we've allowed such an environment to flourish?"

Mother Saunders gazed across the table at her, and Mother Tanner noticed how dark her eyes were, how intense.

"The devil can only hurt you if you're not ready for him," she said. "If you know what's coming, you can look him in the eye, stand your ground and bring him to his knees. It's what women have been doing for centuries."

Mother Tanner laughed and they both sensed an easing of the tension in the room. It hadn't broken completely, but the air no longer seemed as charged as before. Mother Saunders picked at her bread and cheese while staring through the kitchen window at the workers in the field.

"I think I know where Ruth will have gone," Mother Tanner said, reclaiming Mother Saunders' attention. "She'll most likely be in the wood, searching for the man in the field. That's where she thinks he took her baby."

Mother Saunders frowned, imagining the girl aimlessly wandering through the trees. "Is that possible?"

"I don't think so," Mother Tanner said, remembering the man with the holstered gun. "But who among us can really say for certain?"

"Then maybe we should find out for ourselves."

Mother Tanner said nothing. Re-entering the wood, even in daylight, was not an appealing prospect, though she couldn't quite put her finger on why. Was it that she was afraid of what she might discover? It seemed unlikely; fear had rarely immobilized her before. If anything, she had always tried to confront it head-on, though she blushed as she pictured herself cowering in the pantry, the memory a testament to just how rattled she had become after Mother Cullen's appalling fertility ritual.

"That place..." Mother Tanner said, looking through the window at the wood, considering the endless secrets it contained. "There are a million hiding places. We could look for a month and still not find anything."

"Better that we try, though," Mother Saunders said. "We can't just sit back and do nothing."

Mother Tanner sighed and was on the verge of telling Mother Saunders about the man with the gun—the man who had calmly said *Mr. Lynch won't be happy that you're out here*—when a figure raced past the window and began beating on the front door.

"Ma, open up! Hurry!"

Mother Tanner rose from her chair and pressed her face to the window. "It's Alice," she said. "She looks scared to death, Hilda."

"Good grief, what is it now?" Mother Saunders said, easing herself out of the chair. "Probably Ronald having trouble with his back again. Honestly, the man's a wreck. Every time he does a little work, his back hollers that it's time to quit."

She moved towards the front door with Mother Tanner a step behind. She opened it, looked at her daughter's face and knew instantly that the problem had nothing to do with her husband's creaking bones. She grabbed Alice by the shoulders and felt tempted to shake the knowledge out of her before she could deliver the bad news. "What? What is it, child? Tell me."

Alice stared at her mother, her eyes wide and alarmed, before she crumpled and started to cry. "They've found Ruth," she wailed. "They found her, just like she wanted them to."

The Man in the Field

MOTHER CULLEN was hanging from the pulley system of the run-down farm building in which she'd been defiled earlier in the day. Mother Tanner stared up at her body, still dressed in the billowing white robe, and felt a profound sense of disgust, as though this tragic outcome had been inevitable from the start. She could barely look upon Mother Cullen's grey face, her eyes defiantly staring out across the square that had so recently played host to her public and private disgrace. It was hard to know what to say, or even how to react; what possible response could be deemed acceptable in the face of such unnecessary horror?

Mother Tanner turned away, staring for a moment at the uneven cobbles beneath her feet. She felt hollow, as though what was left of her humanity had been scooped out and replaced with a searing pain across her chest. It felt to Mother Tanner like shame.

She heard Mother Saunders beside her mutter the phrase "Lord have mercy", but upon whom or what she wished His blessing remained unclear. Was she making the appeal on behalf of the dead body, still visibly swinging from the hay loft? If so, the plea seemed utterly redundant as Mother Cullen was gone, reduced to this final, grief-stricken lament. Or was the prayer directed at Father Lynch and the Council, she wondered, a petition for forgiveness for the men who had overseen the last hours of this poor young woman's life? Worse still, it occurred to Mother Tanner that the entreaty may have been for everyone in the village, forced to look upon what their apathy had summoned; not the grace of God, but this delicate creature with a rope about her neck making a statement that was impossible to ignore.

Mother Tanner shook her head, feeling a sudden urge to vomit. She closed her eyes and fought it off, determined not to make the scene any worse than it already was. She tried to imagine how Mother Cullen must have felt after the Offering but found that, despite her many years, she had no frame of reference for it. She pictured Mother Cullen—resilient and filled to the brim with moral indignation and rage—escaping the clutches of the Council and taking back her right to make her own decisions, favoring the one choice left to her that no man could possibly affect. She had procured the rope, made her way back to the square and, in an act of willful defiance that left Mother Tanner weak at the knees, had finally left her grief and her baby behind.

There were now a dozen or more people in the square, all staring up at Mother Cullen's corpse, with more arriving every minute. It was an awful parody of the ceremonial gathering, a terrible recreation that Mother Tanner had no doubt was exactly what Mother Cullen had intended. As before, Mother Tanner recognized most of those already assembled, but found it difficult to look anyone in the eye for fear of seeing some repulsive part of herself reflected back. It was a grim thought indeed, made worse by the realization that, by standing here in the square, she was no different from any of the other villagers, all of whom were in some way implicated in Mother Cullen's death. This wasn't just about Father Lynch and the Council; it was about all of them. Mother Tanner knew this implicitly, though what difference it made at this point—if indeed it made any at all—was hard to define.

"We should leave," she said, turning to see Mother Saunders consoling Alice, who looked pale and was visibly shaking. "I don't want to be here when they arrive."

She didn't need to elaborate; she could sense that Mother Saunders felt the same way, and all three of them turned their back on Mother Cullen's enduring accusation—plain for all to see—and silently headed away from the square.

PASSING THROUGH the village, they barely exchanged a word. Alice was clearly in shock and Mother Saunders had to physically support her as they walked, whispering into her ear the entire length of the journey. When they arrived at Mother Saunders' house, there was a moment where none of them knew quite what to say. The pause felt mildly uncomfortable and Mother Tanner eventually just nodded her head and told Mother Saunders to take care of her baby, watching as Alice was gently escorted down the path.

When they were gone, Mother Tanner listened to the silence of the village. The usual sound of machinery and intensive labor was oddly absent and she wondered if news of Mother Cullen's death had at the very least brought the community to a grinding halt. She certainly hoped so. It felt like a seminal moment in time, though what this might mean moving forward she had no idea.

She turned and looked out across the rolling fields to the dark expanse of woodland beyond, the jagged trees in the distance nudging the sky. Had they always looked so ominous? Or had her impression of the place altered only after her unexpected jaunt with Mother Cullen? It was hard to say, yet there was no denying that she felt differently about whatever lay on the far side of the fields. Not afraid, exactly; just curious. She could barely remember even thinking about the woods prior to the events of the last few days. Now here she was considering yet again what those ancient trees might conceal. It was because of the man with the gun, she thought. That was why she couldn't get the damn place out of her head. The man who had firmly told them to leave the woods, insisting *this is not a place for you*. Was he still in there, she wondered, patrolling the border, looking out for intruders and obeying the directive of *Mr. Lynch*?

It seemed more than plausible to imagine that he was. Perhaps he was cleaning his gun or drinking from a hip flask or just standing among the trees staring back at the village and asking himself what in God's name he was doing. What were his duties, she wondered? Short of keeping the area clear she struggled to imagine what else the man had been hired to do. This was a God-fearing place, a community built on trust and tradition that spent its time honoring the land. How many villagers each year wandered freely into the woods and had to be turned back by an armed guard? In all her years here, Mother Tanner had never heard of such a thing. Very few people ever left the village and those that had, like Mother Dalton's daughter, Flora, who had fled last year for the city, did so on the understanding that they would never be allowed to return. That was the deal; the villagers only wanted their own, and those few who rejected their heritage were painfully cast aside.

She tried to think of the last person before Flora to turn their back on the community, but no one came to mind. Most stayed and fulfilled their birthright, working the fields and celebrating the Turning of the Wheel. But *most* wasn't *all*, that was the underlying point, and Mother Tanner wondered if any over the years had managed to escape through the woods. She considered again the man with the gun. He alone couldn't patrol the entire region; it was impossible. But where there was one, she thought, there would always be another, just like the ants that trespassed in her larder during the summer. There would be more men, and more guns. Though quite why this might be the case she still couldn't fathom.

She peered into the dense woodland, trying to penetrate the darkness. Was he in there? Was he watching her even now, daring her to return? Was he smiling as he stared back, waiting to see what she would do next, patient and full of secrets, his purpose forever unclear?

She took a step forward off the path and held her breath, not sure what she was expecting. Nothing, as it turned out. Just more silence. She took another step, and another, until she was walking steadily and with mounting unease towards the wood.

She picked up her pace and slogged across the uneven ground, her heart on fire inside her chest. What the devil was she playing at? If someone saw her heading across the field they'd no doubt report it and she'd be hauled before the Council again. Worse still, she wouldn't have the bubble of Mother Cullen's grief to protect her. It would just be her and Father Lynch, thrashing out the particulars of what went on in the wood, her moral compass swinging one way, his righteous anger another, until they both ended up victims of their own circumstance, tired, conflicted and alone.

She risked a glance over her shoulder and breathed a sigh of relief when she realized there was no one in sight. Still in the square, no doubt, angling for a better view of Mother Cullen's corpse. What a desperate spectacle! Mother Tanner only realized she was weeping when the tears trickled into the corners of her mouth. She wiped her eyes with the back of her hand and pressed on, more determined than ever to discover for herself what mystery—if any—lay hidden among the trees.

She was moving almost without thinking now, possessed only of a single-minded desire to explore what she and Mother Cullen had previously been denied. She reached the boundary fence, lifted the wire and eased through to the other side.

The woodland that stretched before her felt radically different during the day, tranquil and inviting, as though its real face—its midnight face—was reserved only for those foolish enough to stumble upon it in the moonlight. She wondered what duties the man with the gun performed when the afternoon was cool and bright, like it was today, with sunlight occasionally dipping through the dense formation of trees. Perhaps he was a reader, she thought. Or someone who enjoyed the solitude, boring into life's complexities in isolation, no different from everyone else; just a man searching for the answers.

She pressed on, holding her breath as she entered the wood, half expecting the man to appear immediately, much as he had the last time she was here. But she was soon past the first cluster of trees and when she looked behind her, the fence and the field beyond it were only marginally visible as the wood closed in around her. The hairs on her arms rose as the afternoon chill penetrated her cloak. It felt damp and vaguely unpleasant, the ground an uneven sea of moss and exposed roots, the air heavily scented with pine.

Mother Tanner felt her chest tightening the deeper into the wood she moved. Whatever this was, it was starting to feel like a mistake. Behind her there was now nothing but trees; in front of her exactly the same. She briefly considered turning round and going back, having questioned her own judgement on the matter and found it wanting, but a familiar noise up ahead froze her to the spot and instantly stole her breath.

Voices. Directly in front of her; no more than fifty yards or so. She held her ground, her hand trembling as she groped at a tree for support. It sounded like two men, talking freely, laughing, neither displaying a care in the world.

She edged closer, suddenly conscious of the slightest sound in the undergrowth, convinced that her racing heartbeat would be loud enough to give her away. What was she even doing out here? This was madness. She was a woman alone in the woods—a woman with no particular experience—advancing on two strange men. Had she lost her mind?

She dismissed her fear as best she could and inched closer. Lost mind or otherwise, she needed to see. Whatever she was about to confront, let the Good Lord watch over her and keep her safe. Wasn't this why she had entered the wood in the first place? To discover the truth about what it concealed? To find out for herself what truly lay beyond the rim of the village? Well, here it was, she thought; this was what lived on the other side. And as always, it began and ended with men.

She could see them now, their green jackets flashing between the trees. There were two of them as she'd thought, hunched over as though peering at something on the ground. One of them had blond hair; the other was wearing a black cap and looked to Mother Tanner, at least from her slightly obstructed vantage point, like the man she'd seen before with Mother Cullen. They were laughing at something and as she dared herself to steal an extra yard or two, she realized that, beneath the laughter, she could hear a catalogue of tinny shrieks and howls, as though they were listening to a recording of somebody being murdered on a transistor radio.

Mother Tanner stepped to within twenty feet of the men and pressed herself against the trunk of a large tree, too terrified to move another inch. The men still had their backs to her, focused on whatever horror continued to entertain them. In the silence of the wood, the distorted screams sounded utterly harrowing, and Mother Tanner thought again about turning on her heel and heading for home. If this was what existed beyond the village—this tableau of oppressive woodland, dark men and excruciating shrieks—perhaps it was better to remain ignorant. Certainly nothing good could ever come from discovering the source of the men's amusement. She should turn around now and leave, while she still could. That was absolutely the right thing to do. Except, the blond-haired man had moved slightly to the left, leaving a sliver of daylight between him and the man in the cap. Just enough space to see that he was holding something in his hand. A small device, about the size of the man's palm, on which she could see a tiny screen showing moving images. What was that, she wondered? A television? It was no bigger than a postcard so it seemed unlikely. Yet, she could see a blurred image flickering on the screen and hear the awful chorus of moans reverberating around the trees. As improbable as it seemed, they were watching some traumatic performance on the world's tiniest television and taking great pleasure in doing so.

She peered at the screen and felt her stomach churn almost as soon as she realized what it was the men were watching. The flash of white of Mother Cullen's gown as it was torn from her body confirmed it. The men were poring over a televised recording of the Offering on a device the likes of which Mother Tanner had never seen before. She listened closely and recognized the pain and horror in Mother Cullen's screams, screams she'd already heard once today and had prayed never to have to experience again. Yet here she was, in a stupefying situation of which she had no real understanding, bearing witness once more to Mother Cullen's shame, while two strange men sought amusement to fill their empty day by watching the entire ritual on a screen the size of her hand.

The world suddenly made less sense than ever and Mother Tanner found herself wanting to scream. This was too much; it was like she'd stepped out of her real world for no more than five minutes and landed in a place where the dots just didn't connect. She sensed a hundred different questions forming in her head, but her overriding thought was simpler than all of them: *Get out! Get out now. Before they realize you're here.*

She backed up and instantly lost her footing, gasping as she tumbled to the ground. This hideous environment had bided its time and then betrayed her, the two men turning in her direction, instinctively reaching for their guns. The man with the black cap already had his drawn, frowning as he covered the short distance to where Mother Tanner lay rubbing at her ankle and cursing under her breath.

"You," he said. "I've seen your face before."

"And I yours," Mother Tanner said, her eyes never straying too far from the guns levelled at her head. She waved her hand towards both barrels. "Could you point those things somewhere else? You can see I'm unarmed."

The blond-haired man snorted. "You might have something under the cloak. I ain't taking the chance."

The man in the cap sighed and lowered his weapon, indicating for the other man to do the same. After a moment's hesitation, he grudgingly obliged, though the gun remained only a nervous twitch or two away from calamity.

Mother Tanner noticed that the small device had disappeared inside the blond-haired man's pocket and was at least thankful that she no longer had to endure the tormented wailing of Mother Cullen. The noise, though deadened by the device, had been too much, like hearing a loved one scream into a pillow. It suddenly occurred to her that for the two men to be watching the event on the screen, someone present in the farm building at the time the Offering was made must have been recording every agonizing second of it. Who would do such a thing, she wondered? And, more significantly perhaps, why?

"Stand up," the man in the cap said, drawing her back to her current plight. "You tripped over a root. That ankle's likely to swell up like a balloon."

Mother Tanner slowly rose to her feet, conscious of only mild discomfort in the ligament of her right ankle. She thought the man was wide of the mark. She'd been clumsy, that was all; she suspected her ankle would be just fine.

"You shouldn't be here," he said. "I told you before. This place belongs to the Ness Corporation. Trespassing ain't allowed. That's why we're here."

"You need a gun to protect the trees?"

The man smiled. "No, lady. We need the gun to protect the land."

To Mother Tanner's ears the notion sounded ludicrous. The land was no more in need of protection from men like these than she was. And who, or what, was the Ness Corporation? Some kind of ecological preservation group? The name was unfamiliar to her. Whoever they were, the men in their employ seemed determined to keep her out. They no longer appeared surprised to see her; now they just looked irritated that their afternoon amusement had been disturbed.

"Could I at least pass through?" she said. "I'm looking for someone."

"You dumb or something?" the blond-haired man said, scowling. "You already been told. There ain't no passing through or cutting across. This here wood ain't open for business. You need to go back to your own, where you belong. Understand?"

The force of the man's tirade made Mother Tanner take a step back. The man in the black cap held a calming hand across his friend's body and the two men exchanged a look. The blond-haired man retreated in disgust, leaving the one in the cap facing Mother Tanner, his face unreadable. He returned his gun to his holster and stood in front of her, looking like an immovable object.

"You were searching for someone last night too," he said. "You ain't a very good tracker, missus. Might be best if you just moved on."

"Have you seen anyone else come through here? A man, perhaps?"

He hesitated, then shook his head. "Just you," he said. "Twice." He seemed to consider something before adding, "Why did you come back?"

Mother Tanner thought for a moment before realizing she couldn't quite remember, other than that she'd felt a profound impulse to do so. Sometimes, she thought, wasn't that enough? She secretly wished she'd been driven by the same impulse more often, especially when she was younger and the world seemed like a more glamorous place, even for somebody like her.

"I don't know," she said. "I just needed to keep looking."

The man nodded, as though he understood. "You ought to be careful, missus. You might not like what you find."

Mother Tanner stared at him for a moment, trying to figure out what he might mean. Like most people outside the community, he seemed to speak in code, which he assumed she'd be able to understand. His expression, as before, was like stone. He was clearly a man rarely accustomed to speaking to women; she could see him watching her carefully, as though he half-expected her to make a mad dash beyond his reach and into the trees.

"Are you referring to Mr. Lynch?"

He lowered his head, but she thought she caught a glimpse of a smile, or something approaching one.

"You should go," he said. "You've been here long enough and have wasted enough of our time. If you come here again, I'll be forced to take you in. Do you understand?"

Mother Tanner nodded, seeing nothing but a dark calculation behind the man's eyes and a growing frustration. She turned to go before she paused and looked back.

"That woman you were watching," she said. "She was a good woman. She deserved better than to be treated that way. You and your friend should be ashamed."

The man nodded, almost imperceptibly, and waited. Mother Tanner felt inclined to say more, but the man's hand was hovering once again over his gun. She turned and walked back through the trees.

SHE HAD every intention of heading back to the village and attempted to retrace her steps, moving blindly between the pines, less certain of her progress with every step. When she stopped, though, it was not so much because she was lost—though that was very much the case—but because she felt an itch of annoyance as she remembered the words of the man in the black cap: *You ought to be careful, missus. You might not like what you find.*

What discovery was he alluding to? The man in the field? Or something worse, something closer to home?

She glanced over her shoulder and realized that she'd left the two men behind, their voices lost in the dense labyrinth of the wood. There was no reason why her search, such as it was, had to end here. She could circle around her original route, moving wide of where she'd encountered the men, and continue marking out a winding path through the trees.

The man in the cap might be right, Mother Tanner thought. She might not like what she unearthed, but at least she would have done the digging herself. Wasn't this the critical factor? That she hadn't been scared off by the threat of men with guns? At this moment in time—and she couldn't explain why, even to herself—nothing seemed more important or more true. It wasn't about outwitting the men or being brave. It was simply that she had persisted in the face of male authority to do what felt right. This was all that mattered; defying the voice of every man she'd ever heard, whose words were growing increasingly faint inside her head. All those sermons she had endured—Father Lynch's powerful rhetoric and seductive proclamations, the cautionary tales and the warnings—now felt like nothing other than what they were: a cunning means of control.

She paused again to try and gauge where she was in relation to the two men. She could hear only birdsong and the sound of her own breathing. The men were somewhere to the east of where she stood, but she had already lost track of exactly where. All she could really be sure of was that the village was still behind her, immersed in its own trauma from which she felt oddly removed out here among the trees.

She continued to walk, without apparent direction, clear in her own mind that it no longer really mattered where she ended up. It was becoming increasingly obvious to her that her journey into the wood was less about finding the man in the field and more about escaping the suffocating pressure of those she'd left behind. Had she ever really, in all good faith, hoped to find anything beyond the border of the village other than a way to muffle the banalities oozing from Father Lynch? Perhaps not; but the wood held secrets of its own for sure. Mother Tanner sensed it in her bones. And it wasn't just the two armed men and the mysterious Ness Corporation either. There were things here that she suspected were as old as the trees. An inner darkness that no one in the village would consider possible in a million lifetimes, lost as they all were in their private struggle with faith and working the land.

She edged her way through the trees, avoiding stray branches and the occasional boggy ditch, finding her way by touch as much as sight. The wood seemed to be growing denser and a flicker of unease worked its way up her spine as she considered turning back, not at all sure if she had the nerve or the inclination to carry on.

She stopped to give the matter more serious consideration and heard a peculiar noise emanating from deep within a grove of trees on her left. She frowned, waiting for the sound to repeat itself, and when it did she realized it was more commonplace than she'd initially assumed. Despite being deep in the belly of the wood, the noise sounded horribly familiar, like a protracted human groan. Was someone lying injured out here, broken and alone, silently praying to be saved? She tensed and waited, listening. There it was again, exactly the same sound, long and drawn out; if not suffering then almost certainly some form of agonized torment, vainly expressed, with only the trees and the birds—and now her—in attendance.

She darted towards the noise and then stopped as it came again, shocked by a sudden realization, her head spinning at the prospect of what she might discover among the trees. It wasn't pain she was hearing, buried out here in the undergrowth; it was ecstasy. How had she not recognized it as such in the first place? She was listening to someone—a woman, Mother Tanner thought—carelessly grunting towards a climax. She crept forward, afraid of what she might find, her body stiffening in protest as every sinew in her body urged her to turn away. This was not her business; her heart knew it, pounding away in her chest, as did the voice in her head which was like a needle in her brain, sharp and insistent, pressing her to let this particular secret stay buried.

The noises were louder now and more urgent, the rhythm almost mesmeric. Despite her better judgement, Mother Tanner eased forward, more curious than she was prepared to admit. She assumed she was listening to the animal lust of one of the men stationed here to patrol the wood. She imagined him dragging one of his women out here to take advantage of the remote location, where he could take her without fear of being overheard. She tried to imagine what kind of woman would concede to such a thing, but found it impossible to establish any context in which a woman with any shame would comply.

And yet, here was evidence to the contrary. Moreover, the woman was clearly enjoying herself. Those weren't the noises of a soul in distress; they were the wild, liberated moans of real passion. Even Mother Tanner knew that. She remembered it well and felt a vague sense of loss as the sound steadily rose among the trees.

A few more careful steps brought her to the edge of the glade in which the lovers blindly went about their business. She held herself closely to one of the trees, pressing her bosom to the bark, and peered out at the two naked bodies sweating furiously in the center of the clearing. At first, nothing registered, not even subconsciously, she was sure of it; she was too distracted by the tangled flesh before her to look beyond it at what was staring her in the face. In the end, it wasn't the bodies that elicited the horror; it was the items of clothing that had been chaotically shed and discarded among the undergrowth. Each item all too familiar: the dress, the cloak, the white prayer cap. In among these items she could see a black tunic and brown breeches, the simple combination of which was enough to freeze her to the spot. The last time she had seen them had been on Father Lynch as he held court in the square to proclaim the righteousness of the Offering. She had stood beside him and smelt the sweat in the rough fabric. It had reminded her of sour fruit in high summer.

She turned her gaze back to the bodies, both of whom were facing away from her. The man was clearly Father Lynch, bent over the woman and thrusting into her from behind, clawing at her pendulous breasts with large, eager hands. Mother Tanner held her breath and adjusted her position. When she finally recognized the woman she wanted to scream for not seeing it earlier. It was Mother Belfield, face turned to heaven, eyes closed, delighting in having Father Lynch's manhood pressed up inside her.

Mother Tanner gagged and had to turn away sharply, desperately trying to avoid being sick. It wasn't that she was particularly surprised—nothing Father Lynch did had that effect on her anymore—it was that this secret liaison was taking place no more than a few hours after Mother Cullen had hanged herself in the square. It was almost as though the pair were rejoicing in the moment, somehow consecrating the woman's death with this appalling act of desire, as though their hunger for one another had been intensified by what they had witnessed. Could that be right, she thought? Could she believe that even of a monster like Father Lynch? Had Mother Cullen's swaying corpse awoken urges in them that neither party could control?

The notion was disgusting and profoundly depressing. Besides which, this was no tentative first encounter. This was the violent coupling of two souls locked in secret shame. The pair had done this before. Many times, she suspected. She glanced across the glade and felt her skin crawl as Father Lynch arrived at his climax, his face contorting, the muscles in his arms tightening. She turned, no longer considering the consequences, and fled through the trees. She choked off a scream, feeling hot and close to fainting. She prayed as she ran, though it seemed futile; the day had unraveled around her and everything had suddenly changed.

SHE STUMBLED as she ran, her path unclear, knowing only that the village was somewhere on her right beyond the trees. She cared about nothing other than removing herself from the sight she had just witnessed, the disgrace of which was burned into her brain. The wood wasn't making it easy. The trees seemed to coalesce around her, steering her away from her intended direction, pulling at her cloak with sharp branches that reached out like acquisitive hands. She could feel them in her hair and scratching at her face, as though to leave her with one final torment as she fled.

She tried to dislodge the dreadful images of Father Lynch coupling with Mother Belfield as she ran, but their rutting flesh had already found a home in the depths of her psyche and she knew she would be forever haunted by it. The grim vision of Father Lynch's buckled face as he climaxed was an abomination too far and as the image formed in her mind's eye she collapsed onto the ground and vomited into the weeds. Dear Lord, she thought, how easily the known world can fall apart.

She wiped her mouth with the back of her hand and looked around. The wood looked more daunting than at any other time, the trees dark and oppressive, the silence more accusatory than she remembered, as though she had been somehow complicit in Father Lynch's degeneracy.

She spat into the ground, attempting to rid her mouth of the taste of bile. There was no option available to her other than to press on through the trees. She veered right, her instincts still insisting that the village lay in that direction, though her fear of what she might be returning to was already starting to eat away at her. It was a different place now; a colder place. Mother Cullen was dead, Father Lynch's wickedness had been exposed and seemingly knew no bounds, and Mother Belfield had confirmed what Mother Tanner had long suspected: there wasn't a single cell in the woman's body that could be trusted.

She spat again, this time not just to remove the taste of vomit, and used her hands to push aside overhanging branches as she made steady progress through the wood. She was still trying to process what she had beheld in the clearing, but her mind felt clogged with immorality as she fought to eradicate footage of Father Lynch. That white, bloated body arched over Mother Belfield, thrusting away like an animal, mauling the woman's body with the same hands that every Sunday were steepled in prayer.

It was an offence against nature; more shockingly, it was an encounter that she knew would plague her for as many nights as she had left to dream. She had been scarred by it; already she could feel it deep inside her, the image indelibly stamped on her soul: Father Lynch's pale, trembling body, the grasping scoop of his hands.

Where to go once the world has shown you such sinfulness, she thought? Only home. Home would be where she could begin to consider the consequences of what she had seen. Home would be where she could make sense of the darkness that inhabited the world.

SHE HAD been correct. The village lay to her right, and after a number of arduous detours she finally located the wire fence and the field that bordered Father Miller's land. When she saw the houses through the narrow gap between the trees she almost collapsed with relief. It was becoming increasingly difficult to draw breath and beads of sweat were stinging her eyes. Added to this upon seeing the village again were tears of joy, though she felt immensely silly for having been reduced to such foolish sentiment in the first place.

She pulled herself together and made her way towards the fence. Ducking beneath the wire, she began the lonely trudge across the field, grateful for all the familiar landmarks that hove into view as she gradually approached her own home. Once she was inside the house, she locked the door, removed her filthy shoes, slumped into an armchair and cried violently until her chest began to hurt from the sobs. It was an emotional release not just from what she had experienced in the wood, but also from the sense of betrayal she now felt in every fiber of her being. Her whole way of life, the existence she had fought for every single day, had been undone in an instant. Father Lynch—and that disloyal bitch Mother Belfield—had deceived them all. He had made fools of everyone in the village, speaking of salvation in the morning, before scuttling away to rut in a field by night.

My God, how easily they had accommodated him! Were they all guilty of indulging Father Lynch's treachery? Had they each, over time, become enablers, making his hypocrisy possible?

She could barely bring herself to consider such a thing. It was too horrible to contemplate. She sank into the armchair, closed her eyes and thought instead of what needed to be done next. A bath, she thought. That was the number one priority. Hot water and plenty of it to wash away the grime of the day.

She rose from the chair, every joint in her legs already starting to ache, and coaxed her body up the stairs to the bathroom. She drew herself a bath, pouring a handful of colored salts into the water, and watched as steam started to fill the room, slowly making the world dissolve.

Mother Tanner sighed deeply and crossed the landing to the bedroom to remove her clothes. She could still hear the soothing sound of the water mixing with the salts in the bath. She removed her dress, which now smelt faintly of pine trees, lay it on the bed and then felt her entire body go cold. Not because she was now only wearing a nylon slip—though this might have been part of it—but because an envelope had been carefully placed on her pillow, the front panel bearing only a single name: *Helen*.

Her first instinct was to peer into the shadows to see if there was anyone still present in the room. It was a foolish reaction, she knew that even as she was doing it, but it was an automatic response, one that occurred like a natural reflex. A wide-eyed scan of the room followed by a sigh of relief;

everything exactly as it should be. The only inconsistency was the envelope, yet even this was enough to throw her off course. On a day like today, when the world had already proven itself to be a strange and hostile place, even the smallest realignment of the frequency could alter the picture. If the envelope had found its way onto her pillow, then someone had to have placed it there, which meant that someone had been in her room.

Mother Tanner shivered and rushed back to the bathroom to turn off the taps. The bath was half full and looked inviting, but her focus had completely shifted and she barely gave it a second glance. She returned to the bedroom, almost expecting the envelope to have disappeared, but it sat untouched on the clean linen, calling to her; that single name—*her* name—written in black ink in a spidery, unfamiliar hand.

She braced herself and claimed the envelope from the pillow. It felt cool to the touch, like a freshly-turned stone in the earth. She stared at the name, wondering who had written it, half-suspecting she already knew.

Without further consideration, she unsealed a corner of the flap, slid a finger inside and tore it open. She reached in and removed a single sheet of white paper, which had been folded in half. She opened it up and saw no more than a few dozen meticulously formed words, which she carefully read three times:

> I carnt do it no more. Im not strong like you. Father Lynch is not what you think. Hes been raping me since I was 12. Hes the father of my baby. I just thort you shud know.
>
> Ruth Cullen

Mother Tanner felt ice running through her veins as she read the letter for a fourth time, trying to process the appalling information Mother Cullen—*Ruth*—had wanted to impart to her before she made her terrible sacrifice in the square. There was so much contained in the short message that she barely knew what depravity was more shocking, that Mother Cullen had been persistently raped by Father Lynch as a child and been sufficiently terrified of him to keep her silence, or that the man revered by the entire village was the father of her stolen child. Either way, the letter confirmed that Father Lynch was far more monstrous than even Mother Tanner had imagined.

Poor Ruth, she thought! That poor child, living with such horrifying secrets, the victim of repeated abuse by a man who seemed untouchable, protected by his place at the head of the Council. How many others had he done this to, she wondered? How many other women in the village were living with the same guilt and shame that had tormented poor Mother Cullen?

The question left her feeling dizzy, her head spinning at the possible revelation, as she imagined layer upon layer of deceit. She sat on the bed, still holding the letter, and silently prayed for Ruth, feeling a profound sadness that the girl's life here in the village had been nothing but a ruinous sham, reduced to a casual plaything for the odious Father Lynch.

For a moment she felt on the edge of tears. Then she read the letter again and forced herself to keep re-reading it until the threat of tears turned to a rising tide of rage. She forced herself to sit like this as the room filled with darkness, her mind reeling as she considered what to do next. This must be what insanity feels like, she thought. This must be how everything you care about finally implodes and the Turning of the Wheel comes to an end.

MOTHER TANNER scurried down the stairs, the bath forgotten, still clutching the letter from Mother Cullen in her hand. In the kitchen she placed it on the table and set about filling the kettle with water. She was doing these things automatically, barely even registering each individual action, her mind in turmoil as she was beset by a dozen different thoughts.

It would have been impossible for Mother Cullen to have left the note herself, she thought. The timing was all wrong. Mother Tanner had still been in bed—head on the pillow, sleeping soundly—when Mother Cullen had been called for the Offering, and she had been in the house talking with Mother Saunders when they'd received news of what Mother Cullen had done to herself in the square. There would have been no period during which

Mother Cullen would have been able to break into Mother Tanner's house and deposit the letter on her pillow. It was as simple as that.

An ally, then. Someone who Mother Cullen trusted completely, who might be persuaded to do this one thing in the name of friendship; or out of pity, perhaps, for a woman whose life had been visibly destroyed. So few candidates, Mother Tanner thought. Who in the village liked Mother Cullen well enough to take such a risk?

Father Whittaker's face floated into view in her mind's eye. She waited to see if others might join it, but his gnarly features and his alone struck her as the only viable option. He had taken pity on Mother Cullen before and doubtless he had felt compelled to do so again. She paused for a moment, making herself a hot cup of tea. Had he known what Mother Cullen was plotting to do in the square? It seemed unlikely; even Father Whittaker would have balked at colluding in such a forbidden act. The penalty for conspiracy would be catastrophic. She had no doubt about that.

She raised the cup to her lips and sipped at the tea. In all likelihood, Father Whittaker had delivered the letter, unaware perhaps that it would be the final favor he would ever perform for the woman he had invited into his home. Was he aware of the explosive nature of the letter, she wondered? Again, it seemed improbable, though not unthinkable. Mother Tanner examined the matter from every angle. If Mother Cullen *had* confided in Father Whittaker, would he not have felt obligated to take action against Father Lynch? In a world where the evil acts of men were justly punished, she had no doubt this would be the case; but here, she wasn't so sure. To what extent did Father Whittaker's compassion for Mother Cullen transcend his fear of Father Lynch? That was the critical question, she thought. Father Lynch was adored by nearly everyone in the village, but he was widely regarded as messianic by most of the men. To openly dispute this view would place Father Whittaker in a very delicate position, caught between moral obligation and outright terror. Perhaps his solution had been to pass on the responsibility, forwarding the letter to someone he felt convinced would have the courage to take on Father Lynch regardless of the consequences. Could that be it, she wondered, or was she simply over-inflating her own importance in the unfolding drama, trying to draw connections where none existed?

Her head was starting to ache with the complexity of it all and she looked again at the letter on the table. How best to proceed? The picture still wasn't clear, but there was a path that had to be taken here; she just didn't know how to find it yet, much like her experience in the wood.

She finished off the tea, which had now cooled and tasted bitter in her mouth. A fitting accompaniment, she thought, to the day's sorrow.

SHE HAD spent the rest of the evening trying to place the pieces in some kind of order. She had followed each thread to its logical conclusion and had determined that the only real option left open to her at this point was to confront Father Lynch with what she knew. Perhaps she could shame him into confessing his sins before the Council, though in truth her hopes weren't high. The man seemed to exist in a world where humiliation touched only the people he governed; she only prayed that there was a little light left in his soul to finally admit to his wickedness before the Lord.

Having arrived at this conclusion, Mother Tanner had wrapped herself in her cloak, pulled on her prayer cap and set out into the darkness, keen not to put the matter off until morning. Now, some twenty minutes after reaching her decision to speak with Father Lynch directly, she stood outside his front door, hand poised above the knocker, feeling a sudden betrayal of nerves. What if she failed to articulate her case with any kind of conviction? Where might that leave her? She was placing her head in the jaws of the beast here; she better make a damn good job of fighting her corner right to the bitter end.

Enough equivocation, she thought, feeling vaguely embarrassed by her indecision. By God, let the dice fall where they may! She knocked firmly on the door three times, took a deep breath and stepped back.

A light appeared in the hallway and she felt a quickening of her heartbeat as she saw Father Lynch's outline through the glass. When he opened the door, he seemed genuinely shocked to see her standing there, though he masked his surprise skillfully and summoned an insincere smile.

"Mother Tanner. How delightful to see you. Unfortunately, the Council has finished sitting for the day. Perhaps I can make an arrangement to fit you in tomorrow."

"I doubt that would be wise," she said. "This is not for the Council's ears. Not yet, at least."

The smile evaporated, leaving behind Father Lynch's real face, the one she had seen in the wood when he'd been dropping his seed into Mother Belfield: hateful, piggish, intense.

"You should go home," he said. "Whatever you have on your mind can wait. It's been a difficult day."

He made to shut the door, but Mother Tanner stopped it with her hand. "I imagine so. What you were doing to Mother Belfield would have been tiring even for a younger man."

There was a moment's pause as Father Lynch processed what she'd just said, before the door opened again onto a man now reassessing what was before him. He looked curious rather than alarmed, Mother Tanner was disappointed to note, and that counterfeit smile was once again plastered across his idiot face.

"Perhaps you should step inside for a moment," he said, moving beyond the door and waving her across the threshold. She hesitated but then realized she was being foolish. The man would not be stupid enough to do anything to her in his own home; not even Father Lynch was that brainless. She accepted his invitation and crossed into the hallway, noticing that, before shutting the door, Father Lynch had first scanned the darkness beyond the house to see if anyone had observed their initial exchange.

He's afraid, she thought; not of me, perhaps, but of the situation. He knows he's in trouble, he just doesn't know how much yet.

She followed him along the hallway and into a room at the back of the house. It looked like a parlor and contained a roaring fire and several armchairs. There was a clock on the mantelpiece with three faces, which made her think of the various masks Father Lynch wore depending on his mood. Either side of it were two porcelain Russian Blue cats, which looked out upon the world with expressions of weary superiority. Like the clock, they looked very expensive. She vaguely wondered how Father Lynch had acquired them.

"Please," he said, taking a seat. "Make yourself comfortable. You seem to be preoccupied with some urgent matter involving Mother Belfield. Why don't you tell me what it is?"

His elbows were resting on the arms of the chair, his fingers interlaced above crossed legs. He looked predatory, Mother Tanner thought, like a fox catching the scent of a hen.

She chose to remain standing, though her legs felt like jelly; she silently beseeched her body not to betray her.

"I saw you," she said, just about managing to keep her voice even and controlled. "Both of you. Out in the wood."

Father Lynch looked at the ceiling, his hand supporting his chin. "This is most unfortunate," he said. "I had hoped to avoid such a thing. Still, you're hardly a credible witness. You're already under review by the Council. Your claim will be disregarded. You must see that, Mother Tanner, surely. Your accusation will be viewed by everyone as an attempt to smear me, nothing more. The only person it will hurt will be you."

He sounded so calm, she thought, so sure of himself. She felt her mouth go dry as Father Lynch's unblinking gaze awaited her next move; she sensed he would be happy to wait all night, watching her like this, the orange glow of the fire flickering across his shadowy jowls.

"There's something else," she said. "A bullet even you might find difficult to dodge."

For a fleeting moment he looked worried, as though he were trying to sift through all the filth he had been involved in to determine which putrid indiscretion Mother Tanner might have unearthed. Then he recovered and his expression was once again inscrutable, like the surface of an undisturbed lake.

"Please," he said, with an easy smile. "Fire away."

Mother Tanner reached for the words, not at all sure at this stage what was likely to come out. She hadn't rehearsed any of this, had only imagined Father Lynch writhing in discomfort as she reminded him of his catalogue of sins. As she looked at him now, she was alarmed to discover that, far from writhing in discomfort, the man looked positively serene. He was buried in the folds of the armchair with the warmth of the fire making him look like one of the porcelain cats on the mantelpiece, all sleepy-eyed and aloof.

"I received a letter from Ruth Cullen," she said, "just before she hanged herself."

She was pleased to discover that this information did at least make him turn a little pale, even in the firelight. He leaned forward in the armchair, his composure hanging by a thread.

"I thought that might interest you," Mother Tanner said. "It certainly made me sit up and take note. You see, it turns out Ruth Cullen was a child you knew well, Richard, and before she took her own life, it appears she had a few things she needed to confess."

Father Lynch waved his hand in the air dismissively, revealing a look of barely-concealed distaste. "That woman was unstable. She had been for years. Whatever she wrote is utterly meaningless. Lies and slander, no doubt. Not even worth the paper it's written on."

This time it was Mother Tanner who smiled, just a little, at finally striking a nerve, her revelation more than enough to agitate Father Lynch.

"I'm sure that's what you tell yourself to ease your conscience. But the truth is, you abused your position. You took advantage of a child, Richard, repeatedly defiling her and using terror to keep her silent." She lowered her voice, the fire crackling in the hearth, before adding softly: "Why would you do such a thing?"

Father Lynch said nothing; he merely stared into the fire, presumably hoping that the flames would burn away whatever guilt was eating away at his heart. Yet when he glanced up, it wasn't shame that was written on his face; it was a profound sadness.

"If you believe such a thing," he said, "you must be as deranged as the woman who wrote it. Don't you see what she's done? She blames me for everything that's happened, poor girl. This is how she plans to punish me. By making up lies and hoping you will fall into her trap. Just as you have done. It's heart-breaking, really."

Mother Tanner frowned, feeling the ground shift beneath her feet. This wasn't right; not at all. Father Lynch should be reacting as all monsters do when confronted with their own wickedness: by breaking down and staring at the cold reality of their crime.

She gazed at him and he smiled back, easing himself into the comfort of the chair.

"That bullet appears to have been a blank," he said. "Care to try again?"

"This isn't a game," Mother Tanner said. "Neither is it lies, despite your little performance. This is something that happened, right here in our village, under our very nose. No one will be able to forgive you for that. Nor should they. Your time here is up, Richard. If you leave now, you might be able to get out before the women hear about it and tear you apart."

She was breathing hard now and knew that what she was saying was nothing short of rambling melodrama; but, there it was. It was done. She had made it abundantly clear that there was no longer a place for Father Lynch in the village. She only wished she'd been able to control her emotions a little better and articulate her feelings without sounding mentally deranged.

Father Lynch began to laugh, and she felt a powerful urge to drive forward and strike him directly between the eyes.

"Very good," he said, applauding her rhetoric. "You said that with such conviction I almost believed it."

Mother Tanner took a moment to gather her thoughts, feeling a heavy pounding in the center of her head. The man was despicable; the urge to inflict violence remained strong.

"You're quick to dismiss everything in Ruth's letter as lies, and I can understand that. It contains your darkest secrets, doesn't it, Richard? None of which you can afford for your precious Council to ever find out. Isn't that the truth of it?"

This observation seemed to momentarily annoy him and his expression darkened. "I *am* the damn Council!" he barked, thrusting his chin forward, his jowls quivering like dough. "The others are nothing without me, and everybody knows it. Your idle threats in that direction are absurd."

Mother Tanner smiled again, feeling like she had gained a fresh purchase on the stone that she was attempting to lift.

"I'm not so sure about that," she said. "The letter also reveals that you were the father of Ruth's baby, the one taken by the man in the field. What might the Council make of that, I wonder? Perhaps someone should suggest looking into the history of all the babies taken down the years. Who knows what we might discover?"

She watched Father Lynch closely as his face turned crimson, battling to retain a degree of control, his smile closer now to a grimace. He looked like a man wrestling with his own demons, some of which appeared closer to the surface than Mother Tanner was entirely comfortable with. There was a brightness in his eyes that looked like hate.

"Now I know you're getting desperate," he said. "I spoke with the boy that fathered Mother Cullen's child myself, along with Mother Belfield. I'm sure I could dig him up again if the circumstance required, invite him to tell the world what he and the girl got up to behind the cow shed after school. I hear it was pretty unsavory stuff. You know how impure the young can be, Helen, when left unsupervised. Quite unnatural, if you ask me."

This time, Father Lynch's smile was wide and true and again Mother Tanner felt an urge to knock it from his face. No wonder he had become so powerful within the Council, she thought; he was as slippery as soap, gliding effortlessly from one deceit to the next, distorting reality until it conformed to the context that presented him in the most flattering light.

She tried to speak, but realized she had nothing further to throw at him; all the mud and stones she had in her arsenal had been used up. She stood there in the parlor, feeling the heat of the fire, gazing at Father Lynch, grasping at last just how difficult it would be to dislodge him from his position in the village. As for the notion that he might freely admit to his sins, she now felt embarrassed to have even considered such a thing. The man was beyond compunction, his moral compass irretrievably skewed; he had learned over the years that artifice and cunning were the two skills in which he couldn't be matched.

"You see," he said now, rising from the armchair and warming his hands by the fire. "No one in the village will ever believe a word you say, because it's simply too incredible to be true." He turned around and faced Mother Tanner. "Whatever you disclose will sound like nonsense once I'm done humiliating you. There's nothing you can do or say that can damage my reputation. Not even this. You, on the other hand, are a woman with a grudge, just like Mother Cullen. Imagine what I might be able to do with a situation like that?"

Father Lynch clasped his hands together and thought for a moment, teasing out the details of Mother Tanner's public humiliation.

"Your husband, for example, the late Father Tanner, who I'm led to believe by members of the Council had a taste for young boys, which he nightly confessed to Father Wheaks. Think about that, just for a moment. The indignity that might befall you should such an appalling secret be spread throughout the community can barely be imagined."

Mother Tanner was holding her breath by this point, listening to the melody of Father Lynch's voice, the force of his allegation filling her with horror. It wasn't so much what he was saying—though that was bad enough—but the ease with which he was saying it, his blackening of Harold's name taking no time at all to be devised, as though the essence of it had always existed, somewhere in Father Lynch's disturbed mind.

"No one would have any trouble believing such a thing," Father Lynch went on. "I mean, look at you. You have all the appeal of a wet sock. Why, I might even be able to get at least half the village to have sympathy with poor Father Tanner. You're a dried-out old crone, Helen. Your husband fucked little boys because he despised what you had become. Isn't that the awful truth of it?"

"Stop it!" Mother Tanner screamed. "Just stop it right now!" She rushed forward and lashed out at him, but Father Lynch caught her arm and she was mortified by how strong his grip was. His face was close enough to touch and she briefly considered leaning forward and biting into his jowls, eager to leave a lasting impression on the man who had besmirched the memory of her husband. She could feel the outrage agitating her blood and stared into Father Lynch's eyes, his expression unruffled, even as his fingers held fast to her arm.

"You should go," Father Lynch said softly, squeezing the flesh around her wrist one final time before releasing her and moving back towards the fire. "I shall pray for you, of course, and for Mother Cullen, too. She was a fine woman and will be much missed. I will write a suitable tribute and will deliver it personally at the next prayer meeting. I trust you'll be there."

Mother Tanner rubbed her wrist and glanced down to see the shadowy imprint of Father Lynch's fingers on her skin. The fire in her belly had begun to fade and she now felt only a stinging sorrow, a clear sense that she had played her hand and lost. In the final reckoning she would walk away with nothing more than an affirmation of Father Lynch's immorality, knowledge that would be hers alone.

She turned to go, but then stopped, realizing that she had one more dart to throw, not even caring anymore where it might land. All that mattered was slinging it through the air, its flight unpredictable, the mystery of it a final apocalyptic footnote on which to depart.

"I know about the Ness Corporation," she said. "I overheard them talking. I know everything."

Mother Tanner smiled as she uttered this; she knew nothing, of course, not a single thing. The Ness Corporation was just another mystery in a universe layered with them, each more unfathomable than the other, the Turning of the Wheel binding them tighter. This was the pattern of her life—the pattern of everybody's life, she supposed—moving from one complex problem to another, trying to unscramble the most obscure code, even when she had only the vaguest notion of what she was trying to unlock.

She watched Father Lynch closely, gauging his reaction to her latest bombshell. Predictably, perhaps, though she thought she detected an initial flicker of surprise, he was as unflappable as ever. He assessed her with a degree of cool detachment—possibly mildly interested by her remark—before raising his eyebrows and shrugging his shoulders.

"I'm afraid you have me there," he said. "Is that supposed to mean something to me?"

Mother Tanner rubbed at her wrist, which felt like it had been placed in a vice. "I'm sure one day the truth will come out," she said. "About everything."

Father Lynch smiled. "I'm sure it will, too. Have a pleasant evening, Helen."

She hesitated, not sure exactly what to do next, before turning and exiting the room. Father Lynch watched her go. His face flickered in the glow of the fire; first darkness, then light. He closed his eyes, muttered a short prayer and wondered if this was what it felt like to be blessed.

CHAPTER 7

THE sky had turned black by the time Mother Tanner left Father Lynch's house, with the moon lost behind clouds and only a smattering of stars and the occasional gas lamp to light the way.

She walked home along the cobbled paths feeling empty inside, uncertain what to do next. The confrontation with Father Lynch had been a disaster; she had placed herself in great peril having declared her full hand, and had left herself utterly exposed. The Lord alone knew what retribution Father Lynch might have planned in the coming days and weeks. That he was a man of sin with carnal appetites that bordered on the perverse was not in question as far as Mother Tanner was concerned; what troubled her was that he was also more than capable of talking his way out of almost any situation. The rest of the Council routinely deferred to him in matters of faith, and the villagers had long been seduced by his honeyed words at the pulpit. If ever a situation arose where the village was invited to consider her word against that of Father Lynch, the outcome was inevitable. She doubted it would even be particularly close.

There were others in the village who felt as she did, though. Mother Gilmore, Mother Saunders and Mother Glatt all bore grudges against the Council for one reason or another, and she knew they all despised Father Lynch's hypocrisy as much as she did. Might they be persuaded to act against him if she laid it all out for them? The lust, the lies, the depravity; surely that would be enough to enlist them to her cause, if indeed that's what it had become. They were women of God, as offended as she was by Father Lynch's countless abuses of power. If anyone in the village could be prevailed upon to do their duty it was these three women, all of whom Mother Tanner trusted with her life. These were women she had prayed with; they had spent evenings baking together; all three had labored in the fields alongside one another, sweating as they rooted through the earth for potatoes. If they couldn't be counted upon to help, then it was a dark hour indeed.

Rather than wait until morning, she turned up a narrow alleyway and headed for Mother Saunders' house, her blood racing, conscious of how desperate she had already become. Did her chances of exposing Father Lynch for the degenerate he was really rest on the shoulders of three unremarkable women? It would appear so, though perhaps she was underestimating them. Mother Glatt for one was clearly not a woman to be taken lightly. And didn't the Bible teach us that it was the meek who would inherit the earth? Mother Tanner smiled as she walked; she could think of no meeker women in the village than Mother Gilmore and Mother Saunders, both of whom would turn the other cheek before ever considering laying a hand upon another living soul.

Still, these were the cards she had been dealt. Though her options were limited, at best, she felt a renewed sense of hope at the prospect of recruiting old friends.

She stole across the square, keeping her head down, resolutely avoiding looking directly at the place where Mother Cullen had ended her life. She shuffled across the cobbles and veered towards the lane that would ultimately bring her out at Mother Saunders' house. She had lost track of time, but prayed that Hilda would still be up, possibly making Alice a little supper, or preparing Father Saunders' pack-up for the following day's chores around the farm.

She realized as she approached the row of properties that she was holding her breath, all too aware that if the house was in darkness she would be spending a restless night in her own bed dwelling endlessly on her altercation with Father Lynch. Someone up there must like her, though, because a single lamp was burning in the front window of Mother Saunders' house. She rushed down the path and knocked on the door. A face appeared at the window, peering around the drapes. It was Mother Saunders, looking apprehensive. Mother Tanner attempted a smile, but couldn't imagine how it might have looked in the faltering light. Mother Saunders' face disappeared and there was a long period of silence, during which time Mother Tanner felt convinced that she had been abandoned on the stoop. Then the door opened and Mother Saunders, her face cast in shadow, was ushering her into the house.

"My goodness, Helen. What on earth are you doing calling at this hour? Is something wrong?"

As the door closed, Mother Tanner released a long, drawn out breath and had to reach for the support of the nearest wall.

"I'm afraid I've made a terrible mistake," she said. "I'm such a fool, Hilda. Do you think we might be able to talk?"

Mother Saunders nodded and guided her along the hallway and into the front room. Alice was sitting on a stool by the fireside, darning some of her father's socks. When Mother Tanner entered, she glanced up, smiled and then returned to her duty, her hand moving in a steady rhythm in the flickering light.

"Would you like some cocoa?" Mother Saunders asked. "There's some on the stove."

Mother Tanner nodded and lowered herself into an armchair. "Thank you, Hilda. I could do with warming through."

Mother Saunders disappeared for a few minutes and Mother Tanner sat and watched Alice at work. She was a gifted seamstress, if nothing else. She nodded encouragement at the child and admired her technique. In the silence she could hear the distant ticking of a clock.

"Here," Mother Saunders said, returning from the kitchen with two mugs of cocoa, one of which she handed to Mother Tanner. "This'll calm the nerves. I've added a little of God's holy water for luck."

Mother Tanner took a sip and smiled. Whiskey. The good stuff, too. It reminded her of Harold, who always liked to keep a bottle in the pantry for special occasions. This memory of Harold made her slump in the armchair as she recalled Father Lynch's lies, his words rattling around inside her head, tarnishing her husband's reputation with such filth she'd felt an urge to be physically sick.

"Helen? Are you okay? You look a little pale."

Mother Tanner removed her prayer cap and used it to wipe sweat from her brow. Harold deserved better, she thought. They all did. Wasn't that why she was reaching out to Mother Saunders in the first place?

"I'll be fine," she said. "Just a little drained. It's been an unusual night."

She glanced across at Alice, uncertain how much to disclose with the girl in the room, but Mother Saunders waved away her misgivings and took a seat opposite.

"Whatever it is," Mother Saunders said, "I want her to hear."

Mother Tanner nodded, though she had begun twisting her prayer cap in her hands.

"And Ronald?"

"In bed," Mother Saunders said. "Sleeping the sleep of the just. Like all men, apparently."

She smiled, but Mother Tanner felt too far removed from such flippancy to join in. Instead, she gazed into the fire and tried to organize her thoughts. She had no idea what to say or how best to say it. She had already mishandled one sensitive conversation tonight; she couldn't afford to do the same again with so much riding on the outcome.

"Susan and Gertrude should be here," Mother Tanner said. "What I'm going to tell you concerns them too. It's important that we discuss it together."

Mother Saunders' expression turned serious and she nodded her head in agreement. "Alice," she said, turning to her daughter. "I need you to run an errand. Make haste to Mother Gilmore and Mother Glatt and tell them they're needed here at once. Can you do that?"

Alice put her father's socks to one side and nodded. She rose and made to leave the room, before Mother Saunders reached out and grabbed her by the arm.

"Quiet as a mouse now, you hear? No lollygagging. Straight there, straight back."

Another nod from Alice and then she was gone. Mother Tanner heard her pull on her cloak in the hallway and caught the gentle snick of the front door as it closed. The girl had taken her mother's advice to heart: swift and discreet. Admirable qualities, especially in a world governed by Father Lynch.

"She'll be back in a trice," Mother Saunders said. "Always reliable in a crisis is our Alice."

Mother Tanner felt a mixture of relief and dread. She was in the home of an ally, she was sure of that, but she couldn't help worrying about the Pandora's box she had opened. Not only that, she had now allowed a young woman to venture out into the darkness alone. What was she thinking? Despite her years, Alice was little more than a child. To put her at risk—even if that risk was only nominal—was beneath contempt; that the girl had been eager to play her part only made Mother Tanner's guilt infinitely worse.

They sat in silence, neither woman particularly comfortable doing so, but unable to articulate anything at this point other than their own nervousness. The clock out in the hall marked the time Alice was away, which seemed to be measuring more than just the passing minutes. To Mother Tanner's mind, it was also giving a fair indication of the degree to which the two women were slowly moving apart: with each *tick*, a delicate stretching of the space between them; with each *tock*, a subtle pressure in the air. Was she just imagining it, or was she picking up a faint sense from Mother Saunders that her arrival here was an imposition? That Mother Tanner had become a burden to those around her, even to those who felt as she did, the unhappy few who dreamed of revolution in the night?

Mother Tanner stared across the room at her old friend, catching her in profile, wondering when Mother Saunders had grown so old. By the glow of the fire, she looked like a woman who had grown tired of living, flames flickering against skin that over time had become slack, like wax that had begun to melt in the heat. Was this really a woman equipped to take on Father Lynch? Were any of them? Mother Tanner felt a heavy weight descend upon her, pushing her back down into the armchair. It was too late, she thought; they were too old to effect change and Father Lynch was too embedded in the community to be deposed. Wasn't that the harsh reality of the situation? It seemed all too obvious now, sitting here in silence with Mother Saunders. She had overlooked how old they all were, how weary, how utterly bound to their way of life they had become.

Holy God, she thought! She had made a terrible miscalculation. How could she expect these women, these gentle mothers and wives, to give up what they believed in and start over in a different world? It would never happen. *Could* never happen; she was wrong to ever have prayed for such a thing.

She squeezed her prayer cap and made to speak to Mother Saunders, to apologize first and then to quietly excuse herself from the room, when Alice returned accompanied by Mother Gilmore and Mother Glatt.

"This had better be damn good!" Mother Glatt barked. "I was in the tub. Bath salts ain't cheap neither."

Mother Saunders had sprung to life and was doing what she did best: playing host to a gathering of women just like her. Mother Tanner smiled as she watched the dynamic in the room change. Alice resumed her darning, Mother Gilmore lowered herself into Mother Saunders' vacant armchair by the fire, and Mother Glatt presided over everything like a fallen idol, heating her hands by the hearth and railing against the hardship of being dragged away from a relaxing soak in the tub.

Mother Saunders returned from the kitchen with a tray of steaming mugs, which she graciously handed to her guests. She sat on the floor beside Alice and said, "Helen? Why don't you tell us what happened?"

Mother Tanner looked at each of the faces gazing at her, feeling an acute sadness, knowing in her heart that what she had come here to do could never be achieved, no matter how much these women might want to support her. She told them anyway, told them everything; about Father Lynch and Mother Belfield, about Ruth Cullen's letter; she even told them about poor old Harold and how Father Lynch had threatened to dishonor him, if only to stop Mother Tanner from speaking out. There was nothing at this point that she felt she needed to withhold; by this time tomorrow, she'd be gone, and the toxic artifice of Father Lynch would be nothing but a memory. The darkness of their meeting would melt away and she would become someone else, someone whose future wasn't defined by the lies and treachery of men.

By the time she'd finished, the room had fallen completely silent, and this in itself was response enough for Mother Tanner. She smiled and looked at the four other women in the room. Even Mother Glatt—usually hot-blooded and fiercely protective of her friends—stood contemplating what Mother Tanner had just disclosed.

"I came here," she said, "to ask you all to rise up against Father Lynch and do the right thing. The noble thing."

Mother Glatt stood a little taller and said, "And so we will, Helen. We'll do whatever it takes. Won't we, girls?"

Mother Tanner smiled and shook her head. "No. You won't, Gertrude. None of us will. I see that now. I was stupid to think otherwise."

It didn't escape her notice that both Mother Gilmore and Mother Saunders looked relieved.

Mother Glatt frowned and looked deeply offended. "You don't think we can help?"

"Of course you could. But my expecting you to is an abuse of our friendship. We can't bring down Father Lynch, no matter what he's done. He's too powerful. Every one of us in this room knows it. So what do we do? Leave the village?" Mother Tanner offered another weary smile, feeling desperately alone. "It's a nice thought, but this is your home. It's all you know. It's all *any* of us know. What lies beyond the village is the very thing we always sought to guard against. The fact that it got in anyway shows just how powerful the devil can be."

There was another silence in the room as the women considered Mother Tanner's words, recognizing at their heart a simple truth: it would be a brave woman indeed—or a foolish one—who chose to renounce the village and leave.

Mother Saunders leaned over and held Mother Tanner's hand. "I have Alice," she said softly. "And Ronald. It's not that easy..." Her voice trailed off, and Mother Tanner waved away her mitigation.

"I understand," she said. "If I was in your position, I'd feel exactly the same. Your choices are limited."

"What about you?" Mother Gilmore said. "Will you go to the Council?"

Mother Tanner thought about that for a moment before recalling Father Lynch growling *I* am *the Council!*

"That's not an option either, Susan."

Mother Glatt, always the most astute of the women in the room, knelt down on the carpet and said, "You're taking off," the remark a statement rather than a question, as though she'd already calculated Mother Tanner's only viable course of action.

Mother Tanner said nothing, just looked at the faces before her, each of them awaiting her response. They were good women, Mother Tanner thought, and she was jeopardizing their place in the community just by being here. Had this been Father Lynch's intention all along? For Mother Tanner to lead likeminded heretics astray? To bring to ground any woman who wanted to see Father Lynch burn in hell for his crimes? She briefly closed her eyes and tried to remember why she had come, the rationale behind it no longer making any sense.

"Is she right?" Mother Saunders asked. "Are you abandoning us?"

What to say to such a candid question? Only the truth, Mother Tanner decided. "Not abandoning, no. Just moving on. For the good of everyone concerned."

Mother Saunders looked shocked and she heard someone—she thought it was Mother Gilmore—choke back a sob.

"You can't," Mother Saunders said simply. "Where will you go? You'll have nothing."

"A fresh start isn't nothing, Hilda. As far as I'm concerned it's everything. Besides, what's left for me here? I'm finished. Father Lynch will see to that. If I stay, he'll do his level best to make sure I end up like Ruth."

"I'm coming too," Mother Glatt said quietly. "You can't go alone. It's too dangerous."

Mother Tanner felt a sudden pressure around her heart. "I could never ask that of you, Gertrude. Your life is here, with the others."

Mother Glatt was not ready to countenance debate. "You didn't ask," she said. "I offered. My mind's made up." After a pause she added, "They have baths in the city, right?" She smiled and Mother Tanner smiled back, unsure what she had done to deserve such a blessing as Gertrude Glatt.

"That's it?" Mother Saunders said. "You decide to leave just like that, without even talking about it?"

Mother Tanner threw her prayer cap onto the fire and watched it burn. "What's to talk about?" she said. "May hell freeze over if I ever set eyes on Father Lynch again. And may God bless every single one of you who stays."

THERE WERE no drawn out goodbyes, no diversions, no last-minute exhortations to think things through. Just the rigid practicalities of departure. Mother Tanner hugged Mother Gilmore and warmly embraced Mother Saunders, imploring her to keep a close eye on Alice, especially around Father Lynch—not that such a caution was necessary anymore. She and Mother Glatt spent a few minutes making arrangements to leave—within the hour, Mother Tanner insisted; with the decision made, she wanted to wake in a new world, far removed from the influence of Father Lynch. The plan was for the pair of them to return home and grab only what was deemed essential and that could be carried in a small valise. This done, Mother Tanner would wait by the cemetery gates on the outskirts of the village until Mother Glatt arrived in her dilapidated van. They would drive to the bus station in the next village—Mother Glatt happily volunteering to ditch the vehicle by the side of the road—and would take a bus to whichever city had the prettiest name.

It was a good plan, Mother Tanner thought, a *careful* plan; most definitely the right thing to do. That Mother Glatt had agreed to join her was without doubt the best development she could have hoped for, in a night that had, up to that point, been nothing short of an unholy mess.

One more round of hugs on the doorstep of Mother Saunders' house, and then the two women were alone in the cool night air, surrounded by darkness, each wondering how they had arrived at such a definitive point in their lives. Mother Glatt was thinking about the scented water going cold in her tub and Mother Tanner was trying hard not to think of Ruth Cullen and the harrowing abuses she had been forced to endure.

"Thirty minutes," Mother Tanner said, her voice no more than a whisper. "That long enough?"

Mother Glatt nodded. She placed her hand on Mother Tanner's arm, squeezed once and then disappeared into the night. The darkness was suddenly so intense Mother Tanner briefly wondered if it was even there. Yet she sensed the land beyond the limits of her vision, waiting to claim her: the fields, the woodland, the trees.

PACKING HER battered brown valise took all of fifteen minutes. She raided her savings jar and filled her purse with notes she'd been hoarding for a rainy day. Guess this is it, she thought. The rainy day come at last. What a pity everything was happening so fast.

She drew in a long breath and took a lingering look around the kitchen. Was she doing the right thing? Was this really the answer? There was no way of knowing, not yet at least. She walked over to the sideboard and picked up an old photograph of Harold. He was standing in Father Murtey's field, stripped to the waist, young and lean, slick with sweat. He cut a fine figure of a man, no doubt about that. She touched his face through the glass and felt a hollow space open up inside, which had once been filled by his loud voice and generous personality.

"Stand and fight, my love, or start again? What would you have me do?"

The Harold in the photo knew only enough to smile at the camera and she was grateful that he had been spared the corruption of his beloved

Council. He would have despised what Father Lynch had become; might even have openly challenged his rectitude, regardless of the consequences to his own position. She ran her fingers over the black and white image behind the glass, certain that, with a heavy heart, he would have reluctantly advised her to leave.

She unclipped the back of the casing and pulled the photograph from the frame. She lay it on the very top of the valise, before closing it and securing the clasps. Done, she thought. A lifetime's essentials folded away in a heartbeat. She wasn't sure whether she should feel dispirited or relieved.

She had taken her thick winter coat from the closet and now slipped it on over her dress. No more cloaks, she thought. No more robes for worship. And definitely no more damn prayer caps! She blushed at the unspoken profanity, still bound by the covenant that had governed her life for so long. It would take a while, she thought, to be free of the Council's constitution; even then, she doubted that she would ever be truly comfortable indulging in idle blasphemy.

She turned and sighed, determined not to weep for everything she had chosen to sacrifice. One last look around the kitchen. One final inspection, committing her old life to memory. Then out the door and into the darkness. No regrets; no change of heart. Just a ghostly departure in the night.

THE WALK to the cemetery took Mother Tanner past a row of cottages, all of which housed people she knew and respected. In an ideal world she would have been able to march on past without feeling anything at all, but there was little chance of that tonight. Each cottage brought back memories of births and marriages, pivotal moments in the lives of friends and neighbors in which Mother Tanner had been fortunate enough to share. This time, though she tried to fight back the tears, she surrendered to the sadness and wept gently as she moved on through the village that was once her home.

She walked silently past the barns and the outhouses, all of which she had once worked in—plucking turkeys, feeding livestock, sorting grain—until she arrived at the narrow lane adjacent to Father Nyland's farm. Beyond this was open countryside leading to the cemetery that received the community's deceased.

Not far, she thought. Almost there. She prayed Mother Glatt would already be parked up waiting for her; if she was forced to wait, she was afraid her new-found resilience might desert her and the whole house of cards would collapse, leaving her breathless and yearning for home. An outcome she was desperate to avoid.

She stood for a moment, waiting for her anxiety to pass. Instead of open fields stretching before her, there were acres of darkness, rolling towards an unseen horizon. The sky out here was usually peppered with birds, all zeroing in on land enriched with food. Not tonight. Instead, the sky held only a deep plunge into funneled dark, a perspective made more complex by the occasional burnt-out star.

It was into this immeasurable space that Mother Tanner first heard the strident cry of a baby. She froze, believing herself to be confused by the night's events, the village playing tricks on her addled brain. She strained her ears, daring the sound to be repeated, and it was: the unmistakable wail of a child in distress, coming from one of the cottages she had just passed.

She turned around and walked slowly back the way she had come, the back of her neck prickling with tension, knowing already which cottage she would be drawn to by the crying baby. It seemed an inevitability. Mother Belfield had lived in the last cottage on the row for as long as Mother Tanner could remember, and it was from this house that the crying could be heard.

Mother Tanner pulled her coat around her, suddenly feeling the night's chill. Her feet felt heavy and when she tried to move, something seemed to be holding her back. Did she really need to see whatever was in the cottage? Or should she just listen to her heart and press on towards the cemetery and Mother Glatt?

The wailing continued and it was enough to compel Mother Tanner forward, the matter seemingly resolved. She walked closer to Mother Belfield's cottage, listening to the baby, thinking how beautiful it sounded; how sad.

If she had questions—and she did; a countless number—they remained momentarily unexplored as she paced along the perimeter of the cottage before walking up the path to the door.

It was ajar; no more than a few inches, but enough for Mother Tanner to throw it open and enter the cottage unannounced. Her heart had begun to beat a little too fast and the noise of the shrieking baby was now beginning to sound like the mocking laughter of the damned.

"Margaret?" she shouted, her voice shockingly loud. "Are you home?"

Nothing; just the ragged crying of the child, resonating through the cottage. It was increasingly hard to think of it as anything other than a pathetic bleating, though its source was no more apparent even though she was now standing inside the house.

"Where are you, Margaret? It's Helen. I'm concerned about the baby."

Still nothing. Just darkness and the echoing cry of a child.

"This is silly!" she said, feeling a rush of anger. "You must be home, Margaret, there's a baby in the house! Now where are you, for Pete's sake?"

She inched forward, listening, unable to check the rising fear that was growing more palpable with each passing step. What in God's name had she walked into? Where was Margaret? And why was there a baby in the cottage crying for its mother's teat?

She drew to a halt, paralyzed by a monstrous thought: was it Ruth Cullen's baby she could hear? Had Father Lynch arranged for it to be stolen and then hidden it away with the one woman he knew he could trust? She thought on it for a moment, bile rising in her throat. Surely not. The notion was too obscene, even for Father Lynch.

She moved faster now, searching every room in the cottage, desperate to recover the baby, the absent Mother Belfield forgotten. She followed the piercing cry, but the sound was deceptive, bouncing off walls and providing no clear indication of where the child lay. The dark cottage was doing its best to confound her, sending the cries ricocheting from room to room and throwing obstacles in Mother Tanner's path as she navigated each unfamiliar space.

After ten minutes of thorough inspection, Mother Tanner found herself in a room she knew she'd already turned upside down twice before, without accomplishing anything more than a severe bang on the knee. She was breathing hard and her joints were beginning to ache. If there was a baby in the house—*Ruth's* baby—it had found a spot in the darkness to cry where it could never be found. Perhaps for all eternity, Mother Tanner thought. Or until Mother Cullen heard its lament and came back to claim it for good.

She shuddered and felt a sudden inclination to leave the cottage—and whatever ghosts it might harbor—far behind. She hobbled out into the hallway, the baby still crying in the distance, sounding now like it was coming from another cottage somewhere further along the row. She pushed open the front door and scuttled as best she could down the path until she was standing once again in the narrow lane opposite Father Nyland's unploughed land.

She stopped for a moment, trying to recover her bearings, and then noticed something out of the corner of her eye. She gasped for breath, the air cold on the inside of her throat. Standing in the darkness, his feet buried in the soil—as was his custom—was the man in the field, the stranger she had grown to know so well. He was watching her intently, his white suit turned black, his face impossibly vague against the backdrop of the hills and the earth. *His face*, she thought; *I can't see it. I need to see it, just once before I leave.* She moved closer, edging towards the open ground in which he stood. She was conscious of the fact that the baby had stopped crying and the village was silent, as though she had side-stepped reality. Was she hallucinating? Is that what this was? A vision? Or was she ill? The man in the field the first warning sign of wires that had come loose in her head?

She stepped onto the mud and moved to within ten feet of him, her hands reaching out to touch his face. *Just once*, she thought. *Grant me that, Lord, at least. Let me see what was hidden. Just once. That's all I ask.*

The man in the field was practically close enough to touch now, but his face remained maddeningly ambiguous. She fell to the earth and cried out, a howl really, because she knew that when she next arose her chance of touching the man in the field would be gone.

She clambered to her knees and looked out at nothing. As she'd predicted, the man in the field had withdrawn, turning his back on her and disappearing into the dark, their fleeting connection—such as it was—no more than a memory, and an indefinite one, at that. She watched him go and thought about the village and Mother Cullen and Father Lynch. She had come so close, she thought, to knowing what it all meant. The man in the field would have told her. If only she could have beheld his true face.

THE VAN was parked exactly where she and Mother Glatt had agreed: outside the cemetery gates. Mother Glatt hadn't been wrong, either; the thing was practically falling apart. Leaving it to die on the side of the road would be a mercy, Mother Tanner thought.

She hobbled over to the passenger door, feeling like someone was jamming a red hot iron into her knee, opened it and collapsed onto the torn vinyl of the seat.

Mother Glatt gave her a quick, critical appraisal. "Fall down, did we?"

"Something like that." Mother Tanner glanced at her muddy skirt and filthy knees and decided to let Mother Glatt fill in the gaps with her imagination.

"Bring everything?"

Mother Tanner held up her valise.

"Not much to show for a life, is it?" Mother Glatt said, indicating her own small case in the back of the van.

"We're getting out. That's more than enough for me."

Mother Glatt nodded, as though that was all the answer she needed, crunched into first gear and headed off into the night.

They travelled most of the way in silence, neither woman feeling inclined to speak; in truth, Mother Tanner had no idea what she might say. How could she possibly express her gratitude to Mother Glatt for taking such a bold leap into the unknown? It was best left to silence, she thought. The words would come in time. They always did. She just had to give it some thought.

The van rattled along at a fair old clip, surprising them both. Though the ride was uncomfortable—it felt like the springs in the seat were holding her hostage, Mother Tanner thought—they made excellent time, and within the hour Mother Glatt pulled over to the side of the road and parked the van behind a large tree.

"This okay?"

Mother Tanner nodded. What did she know of subterfuge? From this point on they would be improvising, each relying on the other. She looked at Mother Glatt's imposing size filling the driver's seat and smiled; good to know that at least one of them had been designed by God to wage war.

"I'll leave the keys," Mother Glatt said. "With any luck some kid will come along and take it for a ride."

A clever idea; clearly there was more to Mother Glatt than brawn, which Mother Tanner already knew, of course. The woman was a Godsend. She considered this phrase for a moment and realized that it fit the situation perfectly. Mother Glatt had indeed been sent by God. How else would Mother Tanner even have travelled this far on her own?

They climbed out of the van, retrieved their luggage and quietly closed the doors.

"How far to the bus station?" Mother Tanner asked.

"About half a mile." Mother Glatt had already noticed that Mother Tanner was having trouble with her knee. "You manage that?"

"If I have to crawl, Gertrude, then that's what I'll do." They looked at one another, smiled wearily and walked on.

It was a difficult journey, but no more difficult than others she'd undertaken in her life. Women the world over led lives infinitely more challenging; men too, she supposed. But eventually, with support from Mother Glatt, she rounded the final bend and saw the bright lights of the bus terminal, heaving with people.

It would be worth it, she thought. She and her friend would make it work. That was all that counted. It was the beauty of flight, as though she had wind lifting her up, transporting her far away, showing her the value of an endless sky.

"You sure you're ready for this?" Gertrude said.

Helen Tanner nodded and walked into the bus station; exhaust fumes filled her lungs, but that was just fine. This was her new world, and it smelled good.

ACKNOWLEDGEMENTS:

THIS STORY owes a debt of gratitude to Norman Prentiss, a good man and a meticulous editor, who was the first person to find something of real value in this peculiar tale of a small community caught in the process of tearing itself apart. Thanks for all your support over the years, Norm. It's been hugely appreciated.

I'm also eternally grateful to the entire team at Cemetery Dance for continuing to endorse and publish my work. Special thanks to Rich Chizmar, Brian Freeman and Mindy Jarusek, all of whom have been instrumental in helping to further develop my writing career.

I'm especially thankful on this project for the tireless work and encouragement offered by my editor, Kevin Lucia, who has been a stout advocate of *The Man in the Field* right from the start. Here's hoping we get to do it all over again on a different project sometime in the future...

Ben Baldwin, artist extraordinaire, has rapidly become a giant of contemporary cover design and I remain blessed to be able to work with him, always benefitting from his patience, kindness and creative genius.

I'd also like to thank the usual suspects for their love and sustenance, through good times and bad, even when I'm being a colossal pain in the arse, most notably Andrew Jury, Stephen Arnold, Mum, Dad, Anna and Ethan.

Needless to say, without the input of all these wonderful people, none of the crazy stuff you've just read would ever have escaped the bottomless pit that passes for my twisted imagination...

ABOUT THE AUTHOR:

JAMES COOPER is the British Fantasy Award-nominated author of nearly a dozen critically acclaimed novels, novellas and collections, including *Terra Damnata* and *Scar Tissue* from PS Publishing, and *Head Space & Other Uncomfortable Surroundings* and *The Fade* from Cemetery Dance. Forthcoming is the novel *Little Boy*, due to be published by Cemetery Dance in 2023. For more detailed information please visit jamescooperfiction.co.uk.

Made in the USA
Middletown, DE
26 September 2022